SOUL FOOD

STORIES

AN OTHERWORLDLY FEAST FOR THE LIVING, THE DEAD, AND THOSE WHO HAVE YET TO DECIDE

EDITED BY
SALEM WEST & CHRISTEL COGNEAU

2023

Bywater Books

Editors, Salem West & Christel Cogneau

Print ISBN: 978-1-61294-291-1

Bywater Books First Edition: October 2023

Printed in the United States of America on acid-free paper.

Cover designer: TreeHouse Studio

Bywater Books
PO Box 3671
Ann Arbor MI 48106-3671

www.bywaterbooks.com

Jacob Budenz, "Of the Air and Land," previously published in *Tea Leaves* (Ann Arbor: Amble Press, 2023), Pages 21-34.

"The witching hour, somebody had once whispered to her,
was a special moment in the middle of the night
when every child and every grown-up was in a deep
deep sleep, and all the dark things came out
from hiding and had the world all to themselves."

Roald Dahl, *The BFG*

CONTENTS

INTRODUCTION

TO THOSE OF US ON THIS MORTAL PLANE, soul food is about flavor. But more precisely, it's about blending what you know with what you have. It's about claiming history from oppression, and it's about building and celebrating community. It has a heart that beats through the ages, sunshine that warms the spirit, and roots that run deep enough to anchor and comfort those who sit down at its table.

Soul food, we know, is more than the sum of its parts—it is a physical *and* spiritual feast. It feeds the *soul*—all corporeal souls. It connects the divine quintessence within each of us—our personality, life, name, shadow, and heart—to our shared past and present and even future.

Soul food, to boil it down to its very essence, is about generations.

But one must wonder, what does soul food mean to those who inhabit the otherworldly outer plane?

What does it mean to a ghost or a ghoul, to a demon or a fiend? How does the vampire, witch, goblin, or fae fathom it?

Who prepares the feast, and who consumes it?

Who gives of their abundance and who is nourished by it?

Is it shared freely, or is it taken with little or no regard?

Is it steeped in vengeance? What about absolution, revenge, retaliation—or the possibility of mercy?

We posed these questions to our Bywater Books and Amble

Press authors and asked them to tell us the answers.

And answer them, they did.

Anna Burke, Jenn Alexander, Jacob Budenz, Virginia Black, Cathy Pegau, and Ann McMan have joined forces to share their visions of how the otherworldly perceive soul food. Some of the stories are dark and devious; a few are radiantly evil, while the others lean toward the bright and buoyant.

So, please take a seat at our table and feast on these literary dishes that range from the ethereal to the heavenly, from the magical to the mystical through the supernatural. Even into the obscene, shimmering with abominations and shattered nerves.

Come on, sit a spell, and let us feed you.

Salem West & Christel Cogneau
October 2023

THE FIVE YEAR REVENGE AGENCY

by Anna Burke

Served cold since 1697

—Slogan of the Five Year Revenge Agency

MARIGOLD WILSON, OF THE BOSTON WILSONS (not the Connecticut branch, who had cut all ties with the family business in the twenties), finished her last task of the day long after the rest of the university library staff had departed for home. A few student workers remained at the desk, but they paid her little heed, too engrossed in their homework or social dramas to care about the actions of a thirty-something research librarian.

This was as it should be. She took a risk working on family business at the library, but in this instance, the benefits outweighed the potential danger. The library was nearer the restaurant where she was to meet Katherine. The smell of toner faded from her notice as she imagined the evening ahead. No scuffed carpets or fluorescent lights; no snarky emails from faculty asking if she'd completed the research tasks they'd asked for only a few hours before, but needed yesterday; no order forms or student requests so specific she was called upon to aid them in their search for esoteric manuscripts on fifteenth-century German river exports. Most importantly, no secret FYRA briefs to weigh on her mind and conscience. Tonight would be filled with Katherine.

First, though, she had to finish.

She assembled the color photograph, typed letter, and envelope on her desk, careful to align the documents with the desk's right angles. Order and symmetry. The photograph, which crossed well over the border of obscenity, featured an older man and a younger woman in the midst of an extremely compromising position. Personally, Marigold found pegging unremarkable, but she doubted the man in the photo would agree. The brief suggested he was the sort of alpha male who considered sodomy emasculating. The woman was young—definitely young enough to be an undergraduate—but the angle of the photo and the woman's tousled hair obscured most of her features. He, however, was unmistakably identifiable. She'd made sure of that when she photoshopped his face onto the original.

The letter was short. As had been dictated five years ago by the client, it read:

> *Dear Mrs. Flaherty,*
>
> *I'm writing to let you know your husband is a lying, cheating bastard who doesn't deserve either of us. I hope you divorce him and make bank.*
>
> *XOXO*

This would have been more believable had it been a DM, according to their youth consultant (Marigold's niece), but the client had been specific, and it was against company policy to contact the client after the payment had processed. Once the job was complete, she would arrange for a complimentary fruit basket, ostensibly from a random service provider wishing to elicit their business. Nothing transpired in between. Doing so would defeat the agency's purpose.

She wondered what Professor Flaherty had done to earn her client's ire. Infidelity, probably, though she'd been surprised before by the motives clients shared of their own volition—FYRA never asked. This package was designed to humiliate the man and break up his marriage. The reasons behind it were none of her damn business.

The printed photo would seem more plausible to his wife than a digital image, she decided as she folded the letter around the glossy three-by-five and sealed the envelope with gloved fingers. Then she slipped that envelope into a larger envelope for safekeeping and tucked it into her bag for later delivery to Mrs. Flaherty's place of employment, eliminating the risk of interception by the mark.

Satisfied, she wrapped her scarf around her neck, breathing in the smell of warm wool, shrugged into her jacket, locked up her office for the night, and headed out of the library past groups of students settling in for a long evening of studying. The low susurrus of their voices followed her for the heartbeat it took for the doors to click shut. Cool October wind replaced it, whispering as it went about its business.

She inhaled until her lungs ached, then exhaled, a ritual as old as breath. Her ancestors had been breathing good New England air for generations, all the way back to the colonies. They'd taken their first breaths beside sputtering hearths and roadside ditches, and exhaled their last in places just as bleak, save for the few lucky enough to work their way into wealth. Only this blustery dark sky knew of all the events that had unfolded in between.

It was impossible not to think of one particular event on days like this, even as her thoughts chafed to turn to Katherine.

1692. Hysteria. Hanging. And the sister who bided her time, waiting years before she took her revenge on those responsible for the slaughter.

Revenge was always best served cold.

She spotted—and was spotted by—Katherine immediately upon entering the dark restaurant. She'd clearly been watching the door, for her face lit up, and she smiled her easy, warm smile. Let Helen of Troy launch a thousand ships; Katherine O'Connor's smile would have guided all of Ithaka's men safely home. She put lighthouses to shame.

The day's small irritations evaporated, and Marigold murmured a polite greeting to the hostess before weaving her way to where Katherine waited at the corner table beneath their favorite painting, a reproduction of Salvador Dali's *The Temptation of St. Anthony*. The surreal, haunting figures of the temptations matched the eclectic décor of the restaurant, with its glass bicycles suspended from the ceiling, and strange, twisting metalwork. It also complemented the twisting, abstract earrings Katherine wore, which she'd kept safely out of her black hair by piling her curls in a precarious bun. It teetered in profuse glory above her sweet, round face.

"Sorry I'm late," said Marigold as she slid into the chair opposite.

"Only you would consider two minutes late." Katherine squeezed her hand, and Marigold squeezed back, savoring the comfort in that soft grip. She loved Katherine's small, plump hands with their tapered fingers and absurdly painted nails. This week's manicure featured a collection of frogs in silly hats. No one would ever send Katherine a letter like the one in Marigold's bag.

Fleetingly, the memory of her own ex surfaced. Beck had hated the Dali. She had never understood Marigold's fascination, and in the six years they'd been married had only once thought to ask why Marigold was drawn to it. By then, there had been no hope of salvaging their marriage.

"How were the kids for you today?" she asked Katherine.

"Little nightmares, actually. I had to call four sets of parents before lunch. Two kids who aren't normally biters couldn't keep their teeth to themselves, and poor Michael had another accident, and Trisha stabbed herself in the leg with a pencil during crafts. Her mom wasn't thrilled about baby's first stick and poke tattoo."

"You are a constant affirmation about why I prefer working with adults," she said, scanning Katherine's freckled forearms for bite marks.

The server swooped in as she finished speaking, and after taking their drink orders, went over the specials. Marigold, who knew precisely what she was going to order, for it was the same dish she ordered every time almost without fail, watched Katherine listen to the options with the type of rapt attention that took skill.

I hear you, her face said, and *I care about what you have to say, and respect you as a human being.* The server warmed beneath the attention.

"And last but not least," they said, smiling shyly at Katherine from behind a large pair of wire-rimmed glasses, "King oyster mushroom steaks with pesto and our chef's almond aillade sauce, grilled to perfection—or the next best thing—served with a creamy risotto and your choice of salad."

Marigold glanced again at the painting above Katherine's head, some of the chill of the night air returning. She was not looking forward to the case up next in her queue, which she planned to tackle over the weeks to come, and which she did *not* want to think about tonight.

"That sounds extraordinary. Mari, you should try it. I know you like mushrooms."

"I will take the seasonal gnocchi and the house salad," she said, gathering up her menu to hand to the waiter, "but you should try it."

No, she would not be partaking of any mushroom dishes, not tonight, and not for many nights to come.

The Five Year Revenge Agency, or FYRA for those who wanted less of a mouthful, was a boutique affair. The family had resisted pressure to scale up for several reasons, and all of these reasons revolved around discretion. Not every case involved criminal enterprise, but most flirted with legality, and it would not do for a client's mark—or law enforcement—to make any connections that might hold up in court. "Small is safe," her grandmother had always said. She wished she could go see Grandma now; unfortunately, the opportunity for conversation had passed several years and one Alzheimer's diagnosis ago.

Instead, she paid a visit to the new Wilson matriarch.

Aunt Norah emerged from her garden with a basket of warty winter squash on her lap and the retrofitted dirt bike tires of her "outdoor chair" studded with fallen leaves. Dead and drying tomato stalks rustled as she maneuvered around the potted herbs lining the garden path, not that the garden needed more herbs. Medicinal and culinary plants bristled from every curving bed.

"Perfect timing," said Norah. "I was just coming in for a cup of tea."

Marigold took the basket from Norah and wheeled her up the ramp to the wide porch of the old colonial. Norah levered herself from her outside chair to her inside chair with a grunt, wiping dirt from her thighs. "I have what you came for, too."

"I'm in no rush." She followed Norah's cropped gray head into the kitchen, with its painted chickens and bright countertops lined with jars, and rooted around for a tin of tea while Norah put on the kettle. While Marigold waited, she wiped the squash with a damp towel and left them on the low counter for Norah to do what she wished with later. Their green and yellow striped rinds smiled up at her.

"It's a nasty one, then?" Norah wheeled over to her spot at the table and waited expectantly, hands linked together on the table. Her wedding ring glinted dully, as it had ever since Uncle Peter had died of that heart attack over a decade earlier.

Would she and Katherine have that kind of marriage if she ever got up the courage to ask? Nothing like a book burning of a first marriage to make a person altar shy. Katherine deserved someone who would cherish her the way Norah and Peter had cherished each other. Not someone tainted, like Marigold.

"Mari."

"Yes, it's nasty."

"I assumed as much." Norah surveyed her out of wrinkled

brown eyes. "You could pass the case to one of your cousins."

"It's in my queue. I'll take care of it. It's one of Jackie's clients, not mine." They both winced at the mention of her second cousin, who had gone off the deep end and was drying out in a facility in the Berkshires. "Record is sealed."

"As per our contract."

"As per our contract," she repeated, hiding her irritation. The client would never know if she looked them up to get some context. All she needed was their name. "But this could kill somebody."

"It wouldn't be the first time accidents have happened. Will your actions cause harm directly, Mari-berry?" Nora's tone was kind, but Marigold knew better. That kindness covered a skeleton of iron.

"The line between direct and indirect is fine on this one."

"Walk the razor's edge. It is what we do. It is what we've always done. Oh, there's the kettle. Would you mind?"

Marigold did not, of course, mind in the slightest. She flushed the pot, breathing in the steam that wreathed her hands and face, then fixed the tea ball, poured again, and brought the fixings to the table. The teapot—a cast-iron affair with minute chicken legs at the base, evoking Baba Yaga—sat on the wrought-iron trivet; the cups in their chipped saucers waited to be filled; the tiny sugar pot and spoon clung to the side of the teapot like a loyal dog. Ritual mattered. There was a way things were done, and doing so created meaning.

Norah was right. She would proceed as usual.

"I was thinking about proposing to Katherine," she said, changing the subject. "But I'm not sure."

"Not sure about Katherine, or marriage?"

Norah always knew what lay beneath the surface. "Marriage."

"There's no shame in divorce. Not anymore, anyway. We fought hard for that right."

"You and Peter—"

"Had I wanted to divorce that man, I would have. Chicken, if you're afraid things won't work out, then wait."

Marigold tapped her empty mug, willing the tea to steep faster and wishing Norah's pet name for her wasn't quite so soothing.

"I don't want her to know what we do."

"Ah."

Nora lifted the lid off the teapot and checked the color, then poured out a cup for herself and one for Marigold. Perfectly brewed. The tea was the clear brown of Katherine's irises: rich and dark against the white of the mugs. Marigold studied it to avoid meeting her aunt's eyes.

"She's the kindest person I know," she said in a voice almost too low for Norah to hear even with her hearing aid. "And she thinks I'm good."

Norah sipped her tea, the lines around her mouth deepening as she drank. When she finished, she said, "Peter never knew."

This was news to Marigold. "But how did you keep it from him?"

"I told him I went birding."

"And he never suspected?"

Norah laughed dryly. "If he suspected, he let it lie. He was a smart man."

"Beck suspected." She sipped her own tea and savored the burn. "She never called me out directly, but she knew there were things I wasn't telling her. It drove her nuts."

"That girl was nuttier than a hazelnut. Don't blame yourself."

Being married to you is like being trapped in a tomb with a maniac, she'd told Beck shortly before they separated. And it had been. Stifling, cold, and lifeless, with mind game after mind game filling up the spaces where love hadn't grown. How much of that was Marigold's fault? Would Katherine—her darling Katherine—develop that same resentment, demanding to be let all the way in?

Norah must have seen the misery on her face, for she took Marigold's hand. "Vengeance is lonely. But we offer justice when the law fails. Our work helps keep the balance."

"We help bitter wives get back at cheating husbands."

"Sometimes, yes. And we've helped the wrongly convicted, the injured, and the voiceless. If you wish to resign, you know you can, my dear."

Unsaid: *Just like your mother*. Did she want out? For Katherine, yes. But would she want out otherwise, or would the thrill of solving another puzzle—how to get away with X, Y, and Z—win out? She wasn't sure she liked the answer.

—

Katherine was not due to come over until four, giving Marigold plenty of time to make bread. She laid out the ingredients in her small but comfortable kitchen, then grabbed the stone mortar and pestle from a cupboard. The glass jar she'd taken from Norah looked innocuous beside the flour and yeast. Evil often did. Donning gloves and a mask, she tapped the grains of rye in the jar into the mortar.

The pestle, cool to the touch at first, warmed in her hands. People had made flour like this for thousands of years. Maybe longer. And for thousands of years, grain sustained, satiated, slaughtered. Each grind of grain against stone violated ancient precepts, even as it also fulfilled them. She held up a head of rye. Light silhouetted the curved shape replacing one of the kernels. How different was this, really, from witchcraft?

Dali's painting was apt in several ways. The surreally elongated, nightmarish shapes of the temptations must have resembled, in part, the hallucinations suffered by victims of Saint Anthony's fire.

Ergot. *Claviceps purpurea*. The nightmarish cousin of LSD.

She had first heard of ergot in regards to her own relations. Many historians—and she'd read the journals—believed ergot to be one possible cause behind the initial allegations of witchcraft in 1692 Salem. Family lore claimed the ensuing trials had led to the death of the sister of FYRA's founder. Marigold had often imagined what it would have been like to watch one of her loved ones hung to death—first as a morbid child, and later in sympathy and understanding when she doubted FYRA's mission.

Ergot-infected stores of grain caused death, sickness, gangrene, and insanity, and the paranoia and hallucinations associated with ergot poisoning must have seemed like witchcraft indeed. How else to explain such horror, if not the work of the Devil and these who served him?

How else indeed. She crushed the fungus with the pestle. What, then, did this make her? She pondered this as she mixed yeast and water with the flour into dough, and as she kneaded, shaped, and baked the loaf of rye, careful not to dislodge the mask covering her mouth and nose.

Ergot poisoning came in two distinct flavors: gangrenous, and convulsive. She wanted nothing to do with either, let alone both. She hoped whoever was on the receiving end of this revenge truly deserved what was coming to them.

Marigold took the highway exit with a glance at the sky, verifying the forecast didn't call for rain. Gray clouds peered back, but they were the high, rippled clouds she associated with this time of year, not the heavy clouds of autumnal rains.

The second component of the brief was more complicated. She required an underground space, small enough to trigger claustrophobia, yet big enough for a person to have a convulsive fit without too much bruising.

A note on the file read: *client requested a tomb but was amenable to compromise, provided the space meets the specifications.* Good thing, too. This wasn't Paris, where she might have been able to find a secluded location in the city catacombs. Instead, New England had graveyards, which were patrolled. Locking someone in a tomb for three days—the prescribed time—wouldn't go unnoticed without some soundproofing, and that in itself would draw attention. The only tomb she had access to was the family tomb in Andover, and while teenagers did occasionally break in around Halloween, she had no intention of linking the family to the contract in any way.

What she needed was an underground storage room, buried shipping container, or abandoned basement. A basement would be easiest. There were plenty of empty houses with basements or storm cellars ripe for the picking—or making drugs, as was occasionally the case. But the spirit of the law demanded she at least try to fulfill the "tomb" aspect before she resorted to checking foreclosure listings like a common criminal.

Renting a tomb was surprisingly viable, but again, too easy for connections to be made, though she would keep it in her back pocket. No, she mused as she pulled off the narrow road onto an even narrower dirt track, edging into the brush like a giant armadillo and cutting the engine, *this* was in keeping with the spirit.

The car's trunk contained a light backpack with water, map, headlamp, and other miscellaneous supplies, as well as a folded camouflage net. She secured the net around the car, removed her license plates and stowed them in her bag, then did a sweep for trail cameras. Nothing. The car was hidden from the road, looked dumped, and contained no immediate identifying information.

Now came the hard part. She donned the plain black cap and bug net, which would blur her face on any cameras she hadn't seen, and set off, checking her compass against the map. Branches broke beneath her weight as she hiked through the woods carpeting the foothills of the Berkshires.

Satellite data, old geological surveys, and a thread on Reddit had led her to this patch of privately owned woodland. It would have been a gorgeous hike had she been walking for pleasure. As it was, it gave her time to contemplate her level of fitness—inadequate to the task—and her knowledge of local flora, fauna, and fungi—only marginally better. Still, the trees, whatever they were, were lovely in their fall coats, the air was crisp with only a slightly uncomfortable edge of heat, and the squirrels skittering through the dead leaves were the only wildlife she wanted to see anyway.

An hour passed. She paused by a rocky outcropping for water and consulted her map again. She should be close by now. If so, she'd see a stream in the next stretch, and once she found the stream, she followed it a quarter of a mile uphill, and then she'd see the entrance. In theory. Either that, or she was totally lost, and no one would find her body for years. There was a more direct route to the site, but she couldn't risk the exposure. So, here she was, huffing and sweaty and increasingly grumpy.

Few of the cases she'd worked were as dark as this one. In theory, nobody needed to get hurt, but theories were, in fact, theoretical, and not to be trusted entirely.

There. Over the next little rise, she heard the sound of running water. Her pace quickened. Something large crashed through the bush nearby, only to reveal itself to be another squirrel. Her ankle rolled on a loose rock as she flinched, but she caught herself on a tree.

The stream wound through the forest in a wet ribbon, swift and surprisingly deep. The slope rendered walking along the bank untenable, but a game trail ran parallel, and she followed it to the hole in the rock she'd come to see.

This entrance to the abandoned iron mine was a side-egress, and the graffiti was minimal. Only one ancient, battered beer can littered the rubble of the front stoop. A good sign. She inhaled the damp breath of earth rising from the shaft and reconsidered her earlier brilliance. Humans were plains-dwellers, not denizens of cave. The sense of trespass went beyond property law. People didn't belong below ground. It fit the "tomb-like" vibe, though. Perhaps too well. She considered the rocks that had clearly fallen since the mine was abandoned. If she wasn't very careful, it would be *her* tomb.

Her headlamp illuminated the shaft ahead, light sparkling off mineral deposits in the stone and casting long, dark shadows. Cautions from her research chittered at her: never cave alone, never cave without telling someone where you've gone, never this, never that, etc. If the tunnel connected to the main entrance near the quarry, however, as the map she'd found indicated, it would be perfect for her needs.

Or would it? Damp stone slid beneath her boots. Insects skulked, fleeing the light. The air smelled strongly of stone, a smell she hadn't known she could recognize until now. Water dripped into the pauses in her footfalls, and she had to duck to avoid hitting her head on the low ceiling. Could she really condone leaving a person trapped here for three days? It was biblical, and she was of the opinion that what happened in the Bible should stay in the Bible. What if the person panicked and hurt themselves?

Not your problem, she told herself. Except it would be, if Katherine ever discovered what she did for FYRA. It was Katherine's voice in her head that murmured its disapproval, and Katherine's disappointment that stoked the embers of shame in her gut.

A rock scraped her ear, snapping her attention back to the present. Blood shone black on her fingers when she touched the spot. *Damn*. She needed to pay closer attention. The headlamp revealed only the direction in which she pointed its beam. She'd been watching her footing and thinking about Katherine. She needed to cease the latter.

Except that proved impossible. Each step that brought her deeper into the cave made the memory of Katherine burn brighter. If she were here, too, Marigold would feel braver. She pictured Katherine dressed in caving gear—or Katherine's version, which was more "Ms. Frizzle goes caving" than athletic wear—and felt a rush of gratitude that she, undeserving as she might be, was the recipient of Katherine's love.

If Katherine were here, she'd employ a silly accent to take Marigold's mind off the spiders and rockfalls and possible conspiracy-to-commit-murder charges.

If Katherine were here, Marigold would have to tell her why.

Pain lanced up through the heel of her boot and she fell, barking her shin on a rock and skinning her palms as she attempted to catch herself on the walls. The landing knocked a grunt out of her that she was very glad Katherine was not here to hear.

"Fuck." The curse echoed oddly in the shaft. Her headlamp, which the fall had knocked askew, illuminated the ceiling. She corrected it and immediately wished she hadn't. A thin piece of metal jutted from the sole of her boot. She didn't need to remove the shoe to know it had pierced her skin. Her heel throbbed. When was her last tetanus shot? And how sharp must this shard have been to puncture a rubber sole?

Grimly, she gripped the jagged end of the thing and breathed in, breathed out, and pulled. Her shout was quiet, as shouts went, but a shout nonetheless, if anyone was around to hear.

She shoved the shard in the calf pocket of her hiking pants. Looking at it right now wasn't an option, but she might need to show the doctor in case something had broken off in her heel. Then, she closed her eyes. One. Two. Three. By thirty her heart rate had calmed and she no longer worried she'd throw up. By forty, she opened her eyes. A fat, black drop fell from her heel to the cave floor. Fuck indeed.

If she took off her shoe, she supposed she could try wrapping her foot in loose plastic, if she had any. Even then, she was in no shape to continue. Her foot hurt too much, and there was still a chance that even if she pushed on to her destination, the plastic could fail, and she'd leave a blood trail any forensics amateur could pick up.

This cave would no longer serve.

"Oh, you poor darling." Katherine held Marigold's foot in her lap, running her fingers a millimeter above the surface of the bandage covering her foot. "Where, when, and how?"

"Where: the woods. When: a few hours before I called you from the ER. How: I genuinely don't know. Carelessness. Though perhaps carelessness also on behalf of whoever left a shard of metal on the ground near a hiking trail."

"Can you put weight on it?"

"With consequences? Yes."

How could she explain the circumstances? Impossible.

"I'll cook dinner." Katherine rose, patting Marigold's calf, and headed for the kitchen. If only this was their life entirely. She missed the warmth of Katherine next to her on the couch. A couch in a house she'd only been able to afford with money from FYRA. It was a modest home in a nice part of town, set back on two acres of land. Nothing ostentatious. Perfectly middle class, and the Wilsons had some generational wealth tucked in the roots of the family tree. Still, a single woman on a librarian's salary should not have been able to afford it on her own.

Katherine had never asked how Marigold could afford such a home, if it had even occurred to her. She was secure in the belief Marigold was as trustworthy as she, with nothing to hide.

Beck had not trusted. Beck had dug, and she hadn't liked what she found. Marigold did not like owning her own part in the divorce, but she could. Her cat—black, naturally—took advantage of Katherine's absence and leapt into her lap to make a batch of biscuits. She stroked his blocky head and listened to Katherine humming as she shifted pots and pans on the stove, the smell of cooking garlic permeating the house.

This house had been so empty without her. Marigold just hadn't recognized it until Katherine had walked in that first time, several months into their courtship, and lit up the cobwebbed corners of Marigold's heart with her laughter and colorful skirts.

Through the door to the living room to the kitchen, she caught occasional glimpses of Katherine's full figure, short and sweetly rounded and everything Marigold, who was angles and bird bones and edges, was not.

God, but love hurt. She blinked past an upwelling of emotion. What if she'd been seriously injured in that cave, or killed, and Katherine had been left wondering and worrying for however long it took for someone to find her car or her body? What was a family legacy, especially one as full of shadows as her own, to a loved one's tears?

"Can I get you anything to drink? Tea? Water? Wine?"

"I'm okay for now," she said, clearing the emotion from her throat.

"I put the kettle on for myself. Are you sure I can't make you a cup?"

Her cat purred loudly, a sentiment she echoed. Of course, Katherine could see through her unwillingness to inconvenience, and had made asking and accepting easier by simply folding Marigold into her life.

"Maybe a small cup of whatever you're having."

"Coming right up," said Katherine, and the sound of water boiling in the kettle poured into Marigold with resolve.

—

Steel skies hung over Aunt Norah's gabled roof when Marigold pulled into the drive. The garden clung to color, a few shrubs still the brilliant reds of autumn, but everywhere else wore the browns of winter. Gourds and squash guarded the porch from their positions along the railing. She studied them for a moment, until the loaf of frozen ergot rye bread chilled her hands.

"Come in," Norah called from somewhere inside. Marigold followed the voice into the kitchen, where Norah sat looking over the garden consuming the entirety of her backyard. Marigold took a seat at the old table. Nicks from ancestral utensils and dents from ancestral cups marked the surface. Her mother had grown up eating at this table with her sisters.

One was born into a family, but legacy was a choice.

"I take it you have something to tell me," Aunt Norah said.

"I do." Her voice didn't waver. She was proud of this fact, for it affirmed her conviction.

"Well?"

"I am taking a step back from the agency."

"I see," said Norah in her best matriarchal tone.

"I will help, of course, but I cannot complete cases. Research, of course, but . . ." She trailed off, some of her nerve quailing beneath that stare.

"You do not want to lie to Katherine. Is that it?"

Marigold held Norah's stern gaze. "It is."

"Very well. Put the bread in the freezer, and I will call your cousin."

"Thank you."

"Mmm."

She recognized her mother's expression in Norah's pursed lips, wrinkled as they were with age. Her mother had retired early to Florida, ostensibly for the weather. The family knew better. Marigold saw her mother at occasional holidays, but she had always been closer to Norah.

As a girl, she'd helped her aunt in the garden, loving its wildness. As Norah lost mobility, she spent more time there, coming by after school to help harvest herbs and to do her homework at this very table. Norah's children were at college by then, and while Norah never asked for Marigold to help her navigate her changing circumstances, Marigold's cousins always thanked her whenever she saw them.

To disappoint her aunt—was there anything she dreaded more?

Yes. Losing Katherine would be worse.

"I'll come see you again soon."

"Bring this woman of yours when you do. I have a few family recipes I might as well share with her, if she'll be sticking around."

Marigold kissed her aunt's cheek. Norah smelled like sage and perfume and the barest hint of something sour. Familiar, familial smells. What would Katherine smell like as they grew old together? Perhaps now she'd have a chance to find out.

To celebrate, she took Katherine out to dinner, not to the restaurant with Dali and Saint Anthony, but to a white tablecloth joint the next town over. When Katherine asked about the occasion, Marigold said, "Because you deserve it," and Katherine stayed the night.

"You could move in with me if you like," Marigold said later, Katherine in her arms and the moonlight a white glaze over her quilt. "It doesn't need to be full time if you aren't ready, but I could give you a key."

Katherine was silent long enough that Marigold knew she'd overstepped. "If it's too soon—"

"No, not at all." Katherine rolled on her side so that they faced one another. In the darkness, memory painted eyes, nose, and mouth where there was shadow. "I'm just surprised."

"Why?"

Katherine stroked her arm reassuringly. "I love you, Mari. And part of loving someone is accepting them for who they are, and meeting them where they are at. You are one of the most private people I've ever met. We've been together almost two years. In my last relationship, and granted I was younger, we moved in together after only a few months. I wasn't sure when—or if—you'd be ready. I'm honored you trust me." The moonlight illuminated her smile. "Of course. My answer is of course."

Had there ever been someone less deserving of such goodness?

"Mari, are you all right?"

She was not. She was absolutely wrecked with shame, happiness, and relief. Katherine took her in her arms and held her, those small, soft hands stroking her hair.

"I'm sorry," she said when her tears subsided.

"For what?"

"For not being more . . . open."

"Hush. If working with kids has taught me anything, it's that people come in so many more shapes than we permit to flourish. You, my little tortoise, are perfect as you are. Thank you for inviting me into your shell."

———

FYRA, she discovered in the days following her conversation

with Norah, had been a vise she didn't know she'd spent her adult life crushed within. Her chest expanded wider with each breath. She got up early to make Katherine breakfasts and lattes, drinking in Katherine's delighted laughter. At work, she assisted students and faculty with their research gladly, without any judgmental commentary running through her head. One morning, she brought doughnuts in for the library staff. Another saw her jiggling her briefcase, the door, and a large container of homemade pumpkin muffins, which Katherine had helped her bake.

Nothing was more quintessentially New England than late October afternoons, she reflected aloud more than once as the sun teased out the golds and reds of the world and as the promise of cold gilded the evenings.

Katherine agreed. Katherine, who today had texted her an address and the words: *Meet me here after work. I have a surprise for you. Dress comfortably.*

She plugged the address into her GPS without looking further into it than the time it would take her to get there, then zipped home and changed from her work clothes into her hiking pants and a knit sweater.

Massachusetts had a surplus of outdoor events this time of year. As long as Katherine wasn't surprising her with a hayride full of shrieking children, she was looking forward to it—and even that horrific scenario might be tolerable in Katherine's company.

The drive passed without too much traffic. She thanked the gods of small miracles. As she drew closer, however, her buoyant mood shifted. Unease gathered at the base of her spine. She knew this road.

Her skin prickled as she eased down the drive. Stone walls and old trees lined the road, houses interspersed in their midst like ghosts. Ahead lay a dead end.

"You have arrived at your destination. The route guidance will now end," said her GPS.

She parked. Blood rushed in her ears. One hundred years

earlier, in the midst of the Connecticut-Massachusetts Wilson split, the family had purchased ground in a cemetery away from the increasingly populous Salem. Here stood the Wilson family tomb.

Had she ever mentioned the tomb to Katherine? She didn't think so. Sunset darkened the grass beneath the cemetery oaks. No one else was in sight, and she did not see Katherine's car. Perhaps Marigold had arrived first—she was early, after all. She'd wait in the car and give Katherine a call.

No answer. The dread clambered up her spine, chittering warnings. She stepped out into the wind and started walking. Leaves crunched beneath her boots in uneven rhythm. The wind murmured ceaselessly, knocking branch against branch. What had been natural and lovely moments ago now loomed with foreboding. She walked faster. The paved sidewalk stretched ahead, rising over the hill at the cemetery's heart, and then down into a shadowed hollow she knew well.

A light, faint and orange, glowed from the darkness. *Katherine*. She ran. Let Katherine tease her for arriving out of breath, so long as she arrived to discover nothing out of the ordinary. Let the dread now clinging to her limbs and tightening like a noose around her throat be superstition, paranoia, anything but what she feared.

Her feet stumbled to a halt before her mind caught up. No one was here. The light came from an oil lantern, sitting by itself on the decorated lintel of the tomb. Quaint. She halted before it, panting, and looked around. She did not see Katherine. The dark stone of the tomb, engraved with the traditional Puritan death's head, kept its own counsel.

"Katherine?" she called. Only the lantern flickered in answer. Sweat itched beneath her scarf, and she scrabbled at it with clumsy fingers. The door to the tomb hung slightly ajar, the light catching the crack in the slab of stone.

She should get help. Turn back and find a witness. Place an anonymous call to emergency services. She should—

A faint moan rose above the wind, weak and confused. She snatched the lantern and pulled hard on the door. Once inside, she vowed, she would lodge her shoe in the crack to prevent the door from shutting entirely. She heaved again, and the door ground open.

Katherine lay on the floor at the far end of the stone room. The sight of her crumpled body drove all thoughts of traps from Marigold's mind. She dove to her knees beside Katherine and raised the lantern to see her face. Katherine squinted and shut her eyes, turning away. No bruises marred her pale skin, but something had happened. Maybe she'd hit her head while looking at the urns resting in their alcoves, and had fallen.

Marigold clung to that fool's hope and gathered Katherine's hand in hers. She pressed her lips against those limp fingers. Lantern light flickered as the wind gusted into a space small enough to be claustrophobic, but not so small one would unavoidably injure oneself in the event of convulsions.

Katherine tried to speak. The words came out garbled. She wet her lips and tried again, finger flexing in Marigold's hand. Marigold set the lantern down on the nearest ledge and hoped that would help Katherine's eyes adjust. As she set the lantern down, however, she saw the bundle wrapped in white cloth: a bundle approximately the shape and size of a loaf of bread. Katherine had brought it, surely.

But she was not sure. She snatched it up, nearly dropping it, and ripped off the cloth. Within, tightly wrapped with plastic for freshness, was a loaf of dark bread. Dark, like rye.

The door shut with a pained grind. She lunged, her shadow huge and looming, and shoved against the slab with all her weight. The faint sound of chains clinked from outside, followed by the click of a padlock.

Her scream of fury elicited a moan from Katherine. She cut off her shout and sank back to the ground, trembling.

"Mari?"

She pulled Katherine into her lap and hugged her as tightly as she dared without hurting her. Her mind was a screen of static: one long buzz of disbelief.

On the opposite wall, sitting beside her great-uncle, sat two-gallon jugs of water. Enough for a few days. Enough for three days, easily. And each, she knew, contained a dose of appetite stimulator.

The water. The bread. The tomb.

"Mari?" Katherine asked again.

"I'm here. Shh. I'm here." The brief hadn't mentioned kidnapping. This shouldn't have happened to Katherine, never mind the why of it. Her shoulders shook with dry, angry sobs. None of this should have happened at all.

FYRA. She'd wondered how her marks felt when the agency's jaws snapped shut around them, making herself believe they deserved it. The reality was worse. Far worse.

It took almost a full hour for Katherine to come fully to, or at least she estimated an hour based on the temperature drop. Her phone and Katherine's had been blitzed by what she suspected was a micro EMP detonation.

"I have no idea what happened. I'd gotten a coffee, and then things go blank." Katherine looked so small, huddled in the corner like that with her patchwork sweater pulled over her hands. Marigold ached at the sight.

"You were drugged," she said. Drugging was a frequent part of her job, and often the easiest.

"But how did you know where to find me?"

Not a shred of accusation in her words, though there should have been.

"I was sent a text from your phone."

"Oh." Katherine frowned. "I don't understand. Do you?"

Again, she knew the question was rhetorical, even though the words ought to have been uttered with suspicion.

She'd bring the axe down on herself then. "I do."

"You do what?"

"Understand."

Katherine blinked, her eyes round with confusion.

"I know who did this. I just don't know if someone paid them to do it, or if they did it on their own."

"Mari, what are you talking about?"

There—at last, that first edge of doubt in Katherine's voice. Marigold would finally get what she deserved.

"Kat, there is something I need to tell you."

"I'm so thirsty."

Marigold jolted out of a miserable daze. Katherine had listened to her story, and then requested some time to think. These were the first words she'd spoken since.

"It's a trap. I told you."

"Whatever they drugged me with is making me feel sick. I need to flush it out."

"The bread—"

"I can deal with hunger, Mari."

Hearing her name stung, even though Katherine's tone was gentle.

"You can't. Not like this. Not for days."

"Someone will hear us tomorrow."

They wouldn't. She put herself between the water and Katherine.

"I'm sorry. I can't let you."

"What is this fungus again?" Katherine asked as her shoulders slumped in defeat.

"Ergot. It's been described as nightmare LSD, but it's much worse than a bad trip. It could kill you. It could give you gangrene overnight, and you could lose your hands and feet. I cannot risk you eating that bread."

"Ergot." Katherine repeated the word. "You've mentioned that before. The trials, right? Saint Anthony's fire."

"They called it Saint Anthony's fire because it felt like burning, and Saint Anthony's order treated it."

"Why ergot? Your family history?"

"It has to be. Katherine—" Katherine held up a hand to stop Marigold from reaching for her.

"Who knew about your connection, though? Who would

want revenge on you like this? I don't believe it was your aunt. That's too cruel."

She wanted to believe that.

"I don't know. I haven't ever told anyone. The closest I came was Beck, but—" But she hadn't. Beck had confronted her about her secrets, and she'd denied everything, had lashed out as cruelly as she could to shut that conversation down forever. *"Being married to you is like being trapped in a tomb with a maniac."*

A tomb. Ergot poisoning. It couldn't have been Beck, could it? Beck could afford it, though. The law rewarded those who knew how to make it work for them, and Beck had been a bad match but a good lawyer. Had Beck kept digging after their divorce? Could she have discovered how to contact FYRA?

But even if Beck was the money, her family had agreed to it. Norah approved each case personally.

"Mari, talk to me."

"She couldn't have. I hadn't quit yet."

"Who wouldn't what?"

"Norah. She approves the contracts. She wouldn't have agreed to one on me. Beck makes sense. My aunt doesn't. And there was no kidnapping in the brief."

"We both know there are ways around oversight."

Maybe Norah meant this as a test, and Katherine was Marigold's punishment for failing. You didn't work for an enterprise like FYRA without it changing you: revenge served ice cold chilled the server over time.

"I should have broken things off with you to protect you, but I couldn't."

Katherine's lips trembled.

Something in her chest shattered. "I'll get you out of this. I promise."

"We'll get out of this together."

Katherine extended her hand and Marigold seized it like a lifeline. *Together*. Katherine might leave her after this, which she deserved, but for now they were together, and for Katherine she could be brave.

Cold leeched into their bodies from the stone floor where they sat pressed close together to conserve body heat. Talking caused thirst, so they didn't. Marigold dozed. Katherine twitched in her sleep. Hours passed.

She'd expected to hear birdsong in the morning when it came, but sound failed to penetrate the stone. Only the barest hint of light gave away the hour.

"Mari."

Katherine's rasp hurt her throat in sympathy. Her own mouth tasted foul and dry, and she had to pee.

"Yeah?"

"I need water."

"I'm so sorry, baby. You can't." She should dump out the jugs and take away the temptation. Her tongue stuck to the roof of her mouth as she swallowed. *Dump them, Marigold.*

She would. Just not yet. They might have to use the water to dilute the pee they'd inevitably leave in a corner. Besides, if they were not released in three days, they would need the water for survival.

She heard the lie in her inner voice even as her brain tossed out logical reasons for inaction. Like Katherine, she was thirsty.

Thirst turned to hunger. The lantern guttered lower and lower, marking the time with its slow death. Katherine started coughing. By the end of the first full day, Marigold was too.

Katherine's hand touched her knee, jerking her out of the trance-like state into which she'd fallen. She blinked in the low, flickering light. Katherine nodded toward the lantern. When she turned her head, she saw the flame was nearly out. Cold hands pressed against her cheeks. Katherine smiled tremulously, cracking a red line in her lip, and tears glistened as they spilled over her lashes.

I love you, Katherine mouthed.

Marigold's lips threatened to crack, too. *I love you. So much.*

Pause. *I'm sorry.*

I know.

I love you.

And I still love you, Mari. Blood stained Katherine's front teeth. *Whatever happens, never forget that.*

The light went out.

Hunger and thirst on their own, she decided, her rear end frozen and her teeth chattering from cold, were tolerable. Together they were hell. Her abdomen ached and her head throbbed, and she was half convinced she could hear her kidneys shrieking in objection. Worse, her tongue no longer was moistened with the vestiges of her salivary glands, and it *hurt*. Katherine had dry retched several times already. Marigold felt nauseous and dizzy. More worryingly, Katherine's pulse beat erratically when Marigold felt her wrist.

That the drug in Katherine's system had sped her further along the course of dehydration was obvious; Marigold felt her beloved's flushed skin and hated herself strongly enough that she was glad for her own discomfort. Katherine was suffering, and it was Marigold's fault.

Though it was not just her fault, was it? Whoever had put them in here bore the brunt of the blame. A hatred so hot and thick it tasted like blood filled her mouth and burned her gums. She would find the people responsible, and she would end them, beginning with Norah. As for how, sealing them in barrels and burying them alive seemed fitting. She would sit over their graves drinking tea and ignore the muffled thumps and screams from beneath the grass.

Katherine.

Marigold knew what would happen: eventually one of them would break down and drink, and then the other would, too. It was just a matter of when. The longer she could hold off, the less time the appetite stimulator would have to weaken their resolve, and the better their chances of survival.

She would put fire ants in the barrels with Beck and Aunt Norah. No—bullet ants. The vision of her aunt's face twisting in agony, however, didn't bring her the relief she sought. It just made her think of Katherine's face in the same contortions.

Did it even matter who was behind this, when the result outweighed any sense of betrayal or rage? Norah, Beck, both—hurting them wouldn't feel good if something happened to Katherine, because if something happened to Katherine, Marigold would never feel *anything* again.

Katherine's lips moved against her shoulder. With a whistling cough, she said, "Water."

"Okay." Marigold's voiced cracked. "Okay, love. I'll get you something to drink."

The first bite of bread tasted better than anything had tasted in the history of food. Marigold cradled her half of the loaf to her face as she gnawed through the light crust to the soft bread beneath. Normally she didn't even like rye. Now, though, rye was manna, even knowing what it contained.

She tried to make herself throw it all up a few minutes later. Her body wouldn't release its hold on the grain. Katherine was more successful.

"Mostly water," Katherine said when she'd finished spewing up the poison. "I think. I can't see it."

"Keep trying." Katherine had to make it all come back up. "Do whatever you have to do."

Failure would forever taste like bile she knew with certainty when only dry heaves rewarded their efforts—assuming she survived.

Her hand brushed something hard below her knee. Inside the lower pocket of her hiking pants was the shard of metal she'd pulled from her shoe. She never had shown it to the doctor. With this, could she pry at the door hinges enough to loosen them?

She crawled with her hand out toward the light, stopping when cold rock met her palm. Feeling up and down the frame revealed the bottom hinge. She gripped the metal shard as securely as she could and fumbled with the broader end, trying to jam it beneath the bolt. When that didn't work, she resorted to clawing at the bolts with her fingers, seeking purchase on the metal. They did not budge. She kept at it, kicking and hitting and even smashing a metal urn on the bolts again and again.

A cramp doubled her over. She dropped the urn and curled in on herself until the cramp passed, but the ringing in her ears from the sound of the urn continued. Sweat beaded at her temples.

No. No, it couldn't be affecting her yet. She picked the urn back up and moved to hit the bolts again.

Katherine lifted the urn out of her hands and wrapped her arms around Marigold. "Just be here with me."

Marigold nodded. She could do that.

They sat away from the vomit and the piss, huddled in respective discomfort. The sound of their breathing seemed very loud to her. One of the possible symptoms of ergot poisoning was temporary blindness, but no way to tell if that was happening, or if it was just dark. Would she know it was psychosis, if and when it set in?

Someone would let them out eventually. All they had to do was get through this.

And then what? They just went back to their lives? She giggled at the sheer horror of it. How was she supposed to come back from something like this? How could she wake up in the morning and face herself, let alone Katherine, for what she had brought on them?

There was something wrong with her and with her whole family, like a sickness in the blood. They needed to be expunged from the ledger. Katherine would have been safe without her. All the people she'd targeted for FYRA, whether they deserved it or not, would be safe. *She* was the poison, not the ergot.

Expunged, expunged, expunged. Burned. Bled out. Her

fingers scratched at the ground, seeking.

The metal shard nuzzled against them like an old friend.

TILLY'S TARTS

---

by Jenn Alexander

"WE'LL TAKE A DOZEN of the butter tarts, please."

Matilda Tucker smiled across the counter at the two young women. They weren't townies, each dressed in designer apparel belonging in a big city. The woman who'd ordered set her Gucci sunglasses atop her perfectly coiffed curls, while her friend took photos of the shop, presumably to post on the internet later.

"Great choice," Tilly said, her voice as syrupy sweet as the baked goods she was famous for. "That'll be $45.20."

The friend looked up from her phone and let out a short whistle of air at the price, but the woman who'd ordered the tarts didn't blink as she reached into her purse for her wallet.

"Cash only," Tilly said as the woman reached for her credit card. "Sorry." She'd never learned how to use the newfangled credit machines.

At this the woman frowned.

"There's an ATM across the street if you need it."

"I've got cash," the woman's friend said, extending a fifty-dollar bill.

Tilly's hands shook as she took the money and counted out change. Her skin was paper thin and hung loosely over frail bones, but as fragile as her hands appeared, they were still hardworking hands. Every morning it was Tilly herself who entered the bakery at 3 a.m. to stir large bowls of raisiny, buttery filling, and carefully work the cold pastry dough into tart shells.

She never worried about losing customers over things like

her cash-only policy or the cost of her tarts. Her butter tart reputation carried enough weight that she probably could have charged double or demanded she be paid in silver dollars and she'd still sell out by noon.

These two ladies had come early, only about an hour after opening. Smart. The cooling rack, where Tilly's morning work rested, was already nearly half empty. She filled a white cardboard box with twelve of the tarts, and then she handed the box across the counter to the woman and her friend.

"Enjoy," Tilly said.

"Best in Canada is what we've been told," the friend with the cell phone camera said, not hiding the skepticism and challenge in her voice.

"We made a trip up here to try them," the woman who'd placed the order, evidently the more enthusiastic of the two, added.

"They'll have been worth the drive," Tilly promised. "Give 'em a try."

They rested the box on the counter and opened the lid, each taking out one of the tarts.

"Hang on," the friend said, as she extended her cell phone to take a photo of them.

Tilly waited eagerly for them to take a bite. That was her favourite part—watching peoples' *yum faces* as she called them as they took their first bites. It wasn't unusual for people to tell her that they'd driven hours to try her butter tarts. Lilith Lake was far from the beaten path, tucked well away in the wilds of Northern Ontario, and it was hardly worth visiting on its own merit. Tilly's Tarts accounted for approximately 100 percent of recreational visits to the area.

The tarts were *never* a disappointment.

The women simultaneously bit into their tarts, and their expressions were exactly what Tilly had hoped for. Their eyes fluttered closed. The more skeptical friend let out a soft "Oh, my God" around her mouthful of sugary goodness.

The other woman nodded. "They're even better than

what people say."

Tilly gave a sweet little chuckle, as though she didn't know the high level of praise her tarts had received.

"What's your secret?"

Both women leaned forward against the counter, hoping Tilly was about to lift the veil and reveal to *them* the inner workings of her culinary magic trick.

Tilly answered honestly.

"There's no secret, dear. They're baked with soul."

She kept her soul in a glass jar on her counter. It had the consistency of honey and was a soft, translucent green, though there was too little remaining to be able to see any color anymore. It was a finicky thing—not the most shelf stable. It went rancid in the heat, and she'd know because she'd get bitter and snappy. When it got too cold, she grew quiet and aloof. Early on, she'd made the mistake of storing her soul in the back of her pantry, and it was only barely before succumbing to the intensity of the dark thoughts she was having that she had thought to move it into some light.

Tilly supposed it was never easy caring for a soul, but a soul that lived outside of her body had proved much more malleable and volatile than her experience of it *inside* her body had been.

The women finished up their tarts and ordered a second dozen to go, all while the lineup behind them was building.

"They freeze well," Tilly promised. "Just be sure to thaw them at room temperature. Never in a microwave."

She bade them each farewell, as they left juggling both the tarts in boxes and the tarts in hand.

They wouldn't end up freezing their tarts. They'd be devoured sooner than either woman would have wanted to admit. Probably before they reached their destination.

The rest of the morning went more or less the same. Tilly filled order after order, her ego inflating a little more with each *yum face* of the day. Some of her customers were local regulars, but most were out-of-towners, having driven to Lilith Lake for a taste of Tilly's tarts.

They weren't some craze of the moment, either. She'd been enjoying Canadian pastry fame for nearly six decades. She'd baked butter tarts for the prime minister—both the sitting prime minister and his dad back in the day. One of Canada's most beloved rock bands had mentioned them in some lyrical improvising during one of their televised performances. She'd even sold tarts to a certain royal duo during their Canadian honeymoon. Her tarts were not oversold, and her fame wasn't the result of clever branding and social media influencing. They were the real deal.

As usual, they were gone by 10 a.m. Tilly hung her "Sold out. Come back for more tomorrow" sign on the door and went to the kitchen to clean and reset for the next morning.

She wiped down the sugar and flour that had spilled out onto the counter. She swept. She organized the ingredients that she'd need for baking the next day.

Then, she went to the glass jar where she kept her soul. That translucent green, honey-thick substance—her magic ingredient—was nearly depleted. She'd baked her soul into batch after batch of the best-in-Canada butter tarts, and now only a thin coating remained, stretched across the bottom of the jar.

She'd been rationing herself recently, but still, her soul was running out. It would be gone by the end of the week.

Tilly's heart hammered in her throat, and she wiped her clammy hands on her apron. Her circulation was no longer what it had once been, making it so she was always a tad on the cold side, but she knew that the goosebumps that spread over her arms, and the shiver throughout her, were entirely due to fear.

She folded her apron and set it on the counter next to her ingredients for the morning, and she smoothed her hands over the creases in the fabric, as though saying goodbye. She expected to be back in the morning, but death's knocking was growing louder.

She could no longer ignore the thoughts of her mortality or the fear that accompanied those thoughts. She'd traded her soul for some butter tart celebrity, and now she was about to find out what awaited her on the other side of life, be it nothingness or eternal misery.

Tilly pulled on her jacket and stepped outside into the crisp late-fall air to begin the short walk to the cottage where she lived on the shores of the lake. The leaves had almost entirely died off of the trees, and the skeletal branches taunted her, as though harbingers of her own imminent future.

Instead of walking home, her feet, of their own volition, took her to the footbridge by the river, where she had traded away her soul decades earlier. She hadn't returned to the bridge since that day, and she was surprised to find it overgrown with moss, the water below having mostly dried up. It was a small and insignificant thing—barely more than a few solid stones stretching across a patch of grass—which was jarring considering the monumental impact that day had had on her life.

She dusted leaves and debris off the stone bench on the footbridge, and sat in the same spot where she'd sat crying that day, when she'd first arrived in Lilith Lake.

She could almost hear the words, spoken softly and gently, as though they carried on the breeze from back through the years. "Oh, my dear. What's wrong?"

Tilly had sat up and frantically wiped tears from her eyes before meeting the demon's gaze, though she hadn't known then that it was a demon speaking to her. She had looked up to see the most beautiful woman standing in front of her, and damn it if beautiful women hadn't always been her weakness.

"It's nothing," Tilly had said, wiping her eyes as she reddened with embarrassment at having been seen in such a vulnerable moment.

But the demon had held her with an intense and almost-hypnotizing gaze that told her how transparent her lie had been.

"Tell me," the demon had commanded.

Tilly hadn't chosen to open up; the words had simply come. She had told the demon about the joyless marriage she'd found herself trapped in, how Walter's touch made her skin crawl and how her future seemed to suffocate her, and how because she had left with no money and no marketable skills she'd be forced to return the next day.

"And if you decided not to go back?" the demon had prompted. "What would be your dream?"

Tilly had laughed off the question, but when she'd met the challenge in the demon's eyes, she'd found herself opening up about her deepest wish, one she'd never said out loud, not even to herself.

"I want to be *free*," she said. "As a little girl, I used to bake with my mom. I've *always* loved baking. If I could, I'd open a tart shop. It would be a nice life, I think, to live in a quaint cottage, maybe here on the shores of the lake, and own my own little bakery. I could live my life on my own terms."

The words crystallized in her mind the moment she spoke them. Suddenly, Tilly *needed* for that to come to fruition. She couldn't go back.

"I can make that happen," the demon had promised.

Tilly had scoffed, still not realizing who, or *what*, she was speaking with, and the demon held up a hand to stop her.

"I'm quite serious," the demon said. "If you truly want all of that, it's yours."

"Really?" Tilly asked. "How?"

"A simple trade," the demon replied.

Tilly had listened as the demon explained that she would bottle Tilly's soul to be added to her baked goods. They were promised to be the *best ever*, and Tilly was told it wouldn't take long for word of mouth to spread and her tarts to begin bringing in a real income. She'd achieve financial stability. She'd build her cottage. She'd have the life she could not even have dared to dream of.

And although the words were incomprehensible, Tilly found herself believing everything she was being told.

"Your soul's not finite, though," the demon had added. "It will run out one day."

"And what happens then?" Tilly had asked.

The demon had looked at her and given a casual shrug. "Then you'll have given away all of your soul, and there will be nothing left when death comes calling."

Tilly had been young, and her soul had had little value to her in those days, having been damned on numerous occasions: for having sex before marriage, for her lustful thoughts about ladies, for leaving her husband . . .

She had been promised hell already, and the afterlife had seemed impossibly far away, so she had not thought twice about trading her soul to get what she wanted most in life.

The demon had extended her hand, and Tilly had not hesitated to shake on the deal. The instant they touched, hellfire itself seared its way through Tilly's veins, turning her blood into lava, and turning air to ash in her lungs. For a brief, agonizing moment, she'd been paralyzed with terror and regret, and then she'd blacked out. When she'd awakened, she had been handed a large, glass jar with her soul inside.

"This is it?" Tilly took the jar, opened the lid, and dipped a finger into the substance. Based on the green tint, she had expected the taste of spearmint, but it had been devoid of flavor. Even so, she immediately wanted more, and she went to dip her finger into the jar again.

The demon had stopped her. "It's finite, remember. Don't devour it all yourself or you'll have traded your soul away *and* you'll have none left for your tarts."

Tilly had obediently closed the jar, though the yearning for more was so strong it was nearly physically painful to do so. She'd known that others who ate her tarts would feel the same pull for more, and that knowledge settled inside of her along with the realization that, this time, she wouldn't have to go back to her old life and the shackles that came with it.

She'd struggled with the weight of the jar as she'd carried it to the motel where she'd rented a room with all of her savings. She'd befriended a neighbour and asked to borrow her kitchen, where she baked the first batch of her now-famous butter tarts, which she'd sold at a little community bake sale.

From there, her little business had taken off like wildfire. She had quickly been able to open a storefront and then build her dream home on the shores of the lake. Everything the demon had promised her had come to fruition, as she baked away her soul a little more each day.

She only rarely paused to wonder what her life might have been like had she *not* taken the demon up on her deal. She'd have gone back to Walter, likely popped out a few babies against all of her desires, and she'd have grown old and bitter.

Tilly pushed herself up from the bench, her knees complaining as she did so. Hell, or whatever awaited her, didn't sound so bad when she thought about a life with Walter as her alternative.

She'd have traded her soul either way.

She walked home, silencing her *what ifs*. This was the path she'd chosen. She'd live *and die* with that choice.

When she got home, she hung her jacket on the coatrack and fed Sugar, her obese tabby cat. Then she called her neighbour to let him know that she was home and Sugar was fed. She'd made an arrangement with him that if he didn't hear from her by 6 p.m. he would swing by. Her time was running out, and the last thing she wanted was for her cat to starve to death because nobody came to check in.

The rest of her life was kept fairly orderly, so if she dropped dead that minute, there was nothing else to fret much about. She knew some folks might be a bit shocked by her dildo collection, but the thought of their reactions made her chuckle, so she didn't care to preemptively purge it.

She also had no special pursuits to fill her final days. She'd enjoyed her time thoroughly. She'd eaten amazing food, seen amazing sights, and had amazing sex. Everything that would have been out of reach in her life with Walter had become possible. All she wanted with her remaining time was to continue to bake her butter tarts and go out leaving her mark on the nation.

And so Tilly baked and sold her tarts, and each day she scraped the bottom of her jar a little more, trying to get the last drops of her soul.

On the day Tilly knew she'd be baking her final batch she woke up even earlier than usual. She made her bed, a chore she rarely bothered with, and went to the kitchen where she overfilled Sugar's food bowl. She didn't know when or how death was going to come for her, but she had the sinking feeling she wouldn't be returning home.

Sugar purred at the sight of the food mountain and rubbed against her legs. His gratitude was short-lived, however. He meowed in protest when she picked him up and forced him to endure a minute of snuggles and a kiss.

"You've been a good companion," she said as she set him back on the floor.

When she left, she moved to lock the door out of habit, but she stilled her hand before turning the key in the lock, thinking again of the possibility of Sugar starving to death if her neighbour couldn't get into her house.

Then she walked the few short blocks to her bake shop.

She found the demon waiting for her inside the kitchen, tracing a long finger over each of the ingredients she'd laid out at closing the day before.

Perhaps Tilly should have been alarmed, or at least surprised, but although she hadn't foreseen the demon's arrival, her presence felt somehow expected.

"You look the same," Tilly said.

"And you've aged," the demon replied.

Tilly laughed at the understatement. The years had weathered her: stolen the color from her hair and the elasticity from her skin.

Yet the demon gazed on in admiration. "Look at you. So much confidence. So full of pride."

Tilly flushed a little at the reverence with which the words had been spoken.

"You know why I'm here," the demon said.

Tilly nodded, even though it hadn't been a question, and walked to the counter, picking up the glass jar that held her soul.

"This will be my last batch of tarts. Then my soul will be gone."

The demon's lips pulled into a sinister smile as she leaned back against the counter, and Tilly's heart beat so hard in her chest she worried it might shatter one of her fragile ribs.

"Is it going to hurt?" Tilly asked, attempting to distract herself from the fear by beginning to measure out the ingredients to make her final batch of tarts.

"Is *what* going to hurt?"

"Death," Tilly answered, as though the answer should have been obvious.

"Oh," the demon said, as though she hadn't even considered that Tilly might ask that, and she gave a little chuckle before she shook her head. "No. *Death* isn't going to hurt."

The way the demon put the emphasis on the word *death* caused terror to tighten its fist around Tilly's throat, and she was too strangled to ask for clarification.

She measured and stirred ingredients as though on autopilot while the demon looked on. She only paused when it came time to mix the last of her soul into the filling. She reached for the jar, resting her hand on top, but didn't pull it toward herself.

"What if I *don't* add this to the tarts?" Tilly asked. "I could keep this last bit of my soul for myself. Then what would happen?"

The demon did not look perturbed by the question. "Has that not occurred to you before?" she asked, and it was clear from the way she asked that she already knew the answer.

Still, Tilly spoke the truth. "When there was only about half remaining in the jar, I considered keeping the rest for myself, but then . . ."

"Then what?" the demon pressed.

"I was at the height of my career. I didn't *want* to hold back. I wanted to keep going. I wanted my tarts to remain the best."

The demon nodded knowingly.

"I wondered again when there was only about a quarter remaining," Tilly admitted. She didn't explain what had happened. She'd come to the same conclusion that time.

The truth was, there had been many times over the years

when she'd thought about keeping her soul for herself, but she had continued to give it away batch by batch. The end had always been another day away.

"You didn't trade away your soul on the day we made the deal," the demon said. "It's been every day since that you've traded it. You could have stopped once you had your freedom, your business, and your cottage on the lake, but you never did."

Shame burned within her at the idea that she had traded her soul for fame. At the same time, pride for her tarts welled within her, the dueling emotions flip sides of the same coin.

"You *could* keep that last bit," the demon offered, answering Tilly's earlier question. "You won't have much of a soul to hang onto, but you'll have *some* and some is better than none."

Tilly considered the demon's words. "What is going to happen if I bake this last bit of my soul into the tarts?"

The demon leaned back and regarded her, looking less human now and more . . . *hungry.*

"I'm glad you asked," the demon began. "And let me assure you, I plan to be honest with you. I believe entirely in free will."

The demon ran a finger up Tilly's arm, scorching Tilly's flesh with her touch.

Tilly cried out in agony at the searing heat she knew to be a promise of what was to come.

"If you bake your soul into this last batch of tarts, then *I* will eat the tarts that you've baked. You will die, and that last bit of your soul will belong to *me* for eternity."

Tilly wet a cold cloth to try to temper the burn on her arm. "And if I keep the last bit of my soul?"

"I'm not about trickery," the demon answered. "I believe in informed consent. I gave you your soul with the promise that you could use it to create the life you'd dreamed of. I've delivered on that promise. You don't belong to me unless or until you trade away the remains of your soul."

Tilly pushed the jar away from her, but as she did so, she had the sudden instinctual knowledge of what else would happen if she chose *not* to bake her soul into the tarts.

She would bake regular butter tarts that she'd sell and people would eat. There would be no *yum faces* or people turning to their friends to say, "Oh, my God, you have to try these." They wouldn't tell her that the tarts were worth the drive.

She could hear them already. They'd take a bite and say, "Yeah, they're good, but I don't know about the best in Canada."

And when she died, whether it was that morning or sometime in the near future, she'd be forgotten.

Tilly's tarts were her legacy. They had given her life meaning. The demon had been right that she'd made a conscious decision to trade more and more of her soul away each day, knowing what the trade meant. Maybe the consequences had once seemed impossibly far off, but even as the jar was depleted she had continued to choose her tarts over her soul.

The demon grinned through sharp teeth knowingly as she waited.

Tilly pulled the jar back toward her and mixed the final scoop of her soul into her tarts.

OF THE AIR AND LAND

by Jacob Budenz

PERHAPS IT WAS BENEATH THE SPIRITS of the air and the land and the water and the mud to intervene in the lives of Hailey and Ainsley, two white women who co-owned a Southern fusion food truck, but when spirits go on living even after those who see them have been driven away, when the world goes on believing instead in single, all-knowing gods or in the movement of the planets or in the world as a simulation or in nothing at all, such beings begin to grow bored. With little else to do then, they agreed almost unanimously it was for the women's own good.

They'd formed the plan two months before the big day, after a phone call from an anxious bride-to-be who sighed with relief upon finally receiving an answer.

"Hey," came Ainsley's breathy voice, tiny and tinny through the receiver.

"I'm so sorry I've left, like, four voicemails," began the bride-to-be, "and I know things are super up in the air now that you and Hailey . . . well, you know—I mean, I was just calling to say that Zoe and I love your food and, like, of course if one of you wanted to, say, just do it alone, or if it's too painful for both of you, we totally under—"

"We're in," Ainsley said.

The bride-to-be, Lila, blinked. Three mud spirits hung from the unmoving ceiling fan above her by their long, furling tails, so close that their bulbous noses detected the unfamiliar scent of lavender in Lila's brown hair. Humans, they'd discovered long ago, only worried about who or what was behind them and at their feet—axe murderers or palmetto bugs. They rarely looked up.

"Um, both of you?" Lila said. "You really don't—"

"We committed to it," Ainsley said flatly. "Unless you've found another caterer, which I'd understand, since we sort of ghosted."

"No way," Lila lied, her voice going up (the spirits knew she and Zoe had discussed other options but agreed to *hold out a little longer*), then doubled down. "No! We wouldn't even dream of it! Oh, my god, Ainsley, thank you *so* much. Sorry again, you guys—"

"Don't mention it," Ainsley said, and it was unclear whether she referred to the *thank you* or the breakup, but the spirits were not convinced. When Hailey and Ainsley had visited the home of the engaged couple a few months ago, the spirits had sniffed the trouble between them, but they could not come to a consensus about how to interfere before the "lesbian food truck power couple" (as Zoe called them) had left, untouched by supernatural mischief. When the spirits learned through overheard phone calls that the tumultuous pair had agreed to cater the wedding on this land, all had been delighted at the opportunity for some excitement, then subsequently disappointed two weeks later to hear that the women had split up without supernatural interference.

After this fateful afternoon phone call, however, the news that Hailey and Ainsley planned to honor their commitment to work the wedding set the spirit world abuzz. They'd been forced to share their land with humans long enough to know how these things went, how the right sort of circumstance could force two horribly mismatched mates back into one another's arms. They were not about to let that happen, not on their land, land that had been theirs before ever there was a Lafayette, Louisiana. It was not, after all, Hailey and Ainsley's first time breaking up. They still lived together.

That night, the spirits of the air and land all met in what

could only be described as a maelstrom high above the field behind Lila and Zoe's house, where the wedding would take place. They seldom met all together like this, as it posed too great a risk of being seen by day or catching an unsuspecting plane in the chaos of their congress by night, both of which would upset the natural order. The human eye would have seen a swirling, sparking cloud of mud and leaves, water and fire, wind and grass, but the spirits sat serenely within an orb of glassy, obsidian-black walls illuminated by eyes of the spirits of the flame, the glittering skin of the spirits of the stars, and the occasional crackling around the ever-shifting bodies of the spirits of the clouds. What follows is an approximation of the debate, as the spirits of the air and land, of course, would not communicate in anything resembling human speech:

We are against all intervention, argued the only voice of dissent: the spirits of the flame. *It would upset the balance.*

The hobgoblin spirits of the mud exchanged meaningful looks with the mutable spirits of the clouds, with whom they often worked in harmony. All present knew that the spirits of the flame opposed the extinguishing of anything resembling fire, even if the flame between such women as Hailey and Ainsley would prove destructive in the end. Perhaps especially in that case.

And yet, said a glimmering purple representative from the spirits of the stars, surprising everyone (the spirits of the stars, keepers of harmony, seldom stepped in except to arbitrate), *it was you who brought them together around a bonfire years ago, even though it was plain to all present they never would have come together.*

And what spirit of the air and land did not remember that day a year and a half ago? How the spirits of flame, on a dare from the spirits of air, had infiltrated a bonfire in Lila and Zoe's yard to play a new, dangerous game: kindle passion between the unlikeliest of lovers and see how quickly it went up in flames. How incisive, introverted Hailey had glared across the fire at the brash, gregarious, twenty-six-year-old Ainsley, five years Hailey's junior in rainbow platform boots and a bubblegum pink romper who had, according to Lila's whisper earlier, gone "from zero to full lez" after her first hookup with another woman just a few months earlier. How later, as ashes danced from the hypnotic glow of the remaining embers, Ainsley sat with uncharacteristic tranquility and asked Hailey how long she'd been a sous-chef, and she didn't talk over Hailey even once, and Hailey had wondered if she hadn't been wrong about this rainbow-bright punk. How, six months later, when the two first began fighting, they'd opened their food truck in hopes it would bring them closer and build trust between them. How it had accidentally built a cult following, particularly among the burgeoning Lafayette queer scene, but not the closeness or trust the two had intended. How even after their first breakup it kept them in a feedback loop of on-again, off-again, business-partners-and-sometimes-lovers state of limbo. How the aforementioned bride-to-be, Lila, a journalist and aspiring novelist, had remarked to her fiancé Zoe without irony that together the two were a forest on fire that didn't know how to put itself out, but they made a damned good vegan Po'boy.

"Star-crossed," that's what they're calling it, continued the purple spirit of the stars, indignation deepening their dulcet tones. *Do you know how insulting it is to hear humans say this on the land over which we shine each night?*

Do you know what else we heard? What else, what else we heard? chimed the spirits of the water, who most closely resembled large silver salamanders, all overlapping one another in their pronouncements like the currents of a brook. *Do you know what else we heard? Yes, we did! We heard them say this is blessed land. Blessed land! They said it was blessed land, yes, and Hailey and Ainsley met under some blessing, yes! That's what they're saying, yes, it is! Yes! Yes, they said—*

And so, concluded the radiant purple spirit of the stars, their firm celestial voice acting as a dam to the overflowing proclamations of the spirits of the water, *it is most urgent we undo this damage, lest the humans flood our small domain for blessings.*

Lest they believe we would bless such an obviously doomed union. It would be a mockery of our power.

Besides, said a representative of the spirits of the mud, daring to articulate what was on all the spirits' minds, who had been confined to a mere fifty acres of land, at the heart of which sat Zoe and Lila's little property where Hailey and Ainsley would cater their wedding, *When's the last time we had any real fun?*

The spirits of flame yielded without another complaint, leading some spirits to wonder whether these agents of mischief and destruction hadn't set Hailey and Ainsley's ill-fated relationship in motion for exactly this purpose. After all, they'd done nothing to encourage or discourage the union of the brides-to-be, reasoning that the two held a flame true enough they dared not pollute it. However, none bothered to question them too closely, for all agreed the relationship must be stopped—for the good of Hailey and Ainsley, for the restoration of the natural order, for the risk of cheapening the mystical reputation of their land, or simply for the allure of putting their underused talents toward some much-needed entertainment.

Over the weeks leading up to the wedding, the spirits of the water dragged the runoff from heavy rains toward the ditch at the end of the property, a little at a time. They were careful not to make the whole property into a mire, working with the spirits of the mud and the clouds not to ruin the entire wedding. The brides, though less than the indigenous people who once occupied the land, did make some effort to acknowledge the unseen forces around them. The spirits were not especially inclined to ruin *their* relationship.

At the start of the big event, although Hailey and Ainsley had shakily agreed not only to cater the wedding but also to "try things out one last time" (a phrase they'd used the last time they'd gotten back together, according to Lila's most recent sources of gossip), the spirits wondered how much incorporeal assistance Hailey and Ainsley would really need to confirm that any relationship between them, romantic or business or otherwise, would be doomed to fail. It was perfect weather for a Louisiana spring—the spirits of the sunbeams and the air made sure it was neither too hot nor too windy, but instead, pleasant warmth reigned while a mild, consistent breeze blew. However, this was largely where supernatural assistance ceased, at first: in the cultivation of the kind of day that would make any homosexuals in their late twenties to early thirties seethe with envy.

Lila and Zoe exchanged thoughtful and original vows beneath an enormous and wise-looking oak (in reality, the squat little golem-like spirits that inhabited it were more cunning than wise). The brides walked down the aisle toward the tree to a live, mellow synth-pop cover of Björk's "Hyperballad" (of *course* the spirits knew who Björk was, and knew that the couple, like many other young, anxious queers, considered this to be "their" song). In lieu of a sermon, a friend of the brides gave a brief tribal history of the land upon which they stood ("This was sacred land," the large man began, and the watching spirits bristled at the word "was" coming from this man who, for all his apparent cultural awareness, still refused to see them). The reception took place beneath a large tent hung with string lights, just outside of which several rented consignment couches surrounded firepits (in which, later in the night, the spirits of the flame would dance, licking occasionally at the hands of party guests too drunk to notice the blisters forming).

In short, the spirits initially wondered whether, even without their intervention, there was any way Hailey and Ainsley could witness such a majestic confluence of love and think their tense, passive-aggressive exchanges could ever hope to lead them to the same.

Still, needful or not, the spirits intervened. Whereas the air outside Hailey and Ainsley's food truck was crisp and breezy, the spirits of the air ensured no pleasant wind flowed through the open windows of the sweltering vessel; the spirits of the flame roared hot and unwieldy on the grills within; and the spirits of the sunbeams beat silently upon the shiny aluminum roof so that the tiny space felt all the more stifling. When either Hailey or Ainsley left to refill buffet trays, out in the breeze, each could not help but sigh at the relief of getting away from the other. Their food truck became a prison, and the already tense interactions between a broken-up-then-maybe-back-together couple working together in the supreme heat turned downright snappy. Outside, the happily wedded couple danced serenely to the tears and cheers of their loved ones.

"White people dancing," remarked Ainsley with a cruel smirk at the bride, Lila, stumbling momentarily over her own feet on the spongy grass, Zoe catching her gallantly.

"You know criticizing other white people doesn't make you any less white," replied Hailey, though the creases at the grin she tried to hide suggested that she'd been thinking it too. She flipped the fried rice on the griddle and said, almost as an afterthought, "It doesn't make you exempt from examining your own privilege, either."

The spirits of the mud, who clung to the windowsill outside of the food truck with tiny claws one would only see with a discriminating squint, snickered amongst themselves. They, too, had been playing their part clinging to Hailey and Ainsley's shoes. Though the ground was no wetter than usual for April in Lafayette, the wedding guests found their shoes surprisingly unsoiled while the floor of the food truck was splotched with slippery earth. But the spirits of the mud would have their real moment soon.

In the meantime, the spirits of the air delivered one swift, whooshing gust through the window that knocked the half-opened cayenne pepper into the bubbling pot of curried vegetables. The rush of air did not linger long enough to cool the cramped space.

"Really?" Ainsley snapped at Hailey, whose job it was to mix and watch the curry and who had yelped at the spill—and, yes, whom Ainsley clearly hadn't forgiven for criticizing her joke moments before.

"It was the wind!" moaned Hailey helplessly, dumping their last can of coconut milk into the brew to offset the heap of spice that had sunken into the mix of swimming vegetables before it could be scooped out. This remaining can, it was clear, would not be enough to undo the damage.

"And we just leave the lid off our spices now?" said Ainsley, not looking up from her chopping.

Of course, it had been a web-like spirit of the grass that had crept up beside the spirits of the mud and curled one of its tendrils around the lid, twisting, while another spirit of the grass had held the container firmly in place with its own tendril. But since the lid had already fallen to the muddy floor where the spice jar had rolled from the windowsill to join it, the two women would never suspect divine intervention even if they'd known how to look for it.

Thus, the rumblings began, even from the most gastronomically adventurous of the guests, that the curry was too spicy. Some, who knew a thing or two about Hailey and Ainsley's situation, even giggled guiltily to themselves about the over-spiced curry, giving variations on, *That's what you get when you hire a pair of fiery on-again, off-again girlfriends to cater a wedding—they fight, and they over-spice the curry.* One guest turned mock-serious at the giggling and murmured that perhaps Hailey and Ainsley had over-spiced the curry in a small, bitter gesture of defiance at the newlywed couple's happiness. The married couple continued to dance, feeding one another dinner rolls, apparently unaware of the spice saga unfolding at the edge of their tent.

It is a marvel what the right kind of wind can carry. The spirits of the air, always listening, snatched the juiciest tidbits of these hushed conversations and slithered as fast as striking cottonmouths toward the food truck windows. As the sun sank, doing nothing to mitigate the oppressive heat inside the traveling kitchen, the spirits of the air subjected Hailey and Ainsley to snatches of conversation about their crumbling ("Yet again!") relationship.

"A shame," they eventually heard *Lila,* of all people, replying to some busybody who was filling her in on the miserable state of the fallen-from-grace lesbian food truck power couple in their hot, slippery food truck. *Fucking Lila*, who had paused from dancing in her sweat-soaked wedding dress. But what must have stung most, the spirits agreed, was the sincerity in her voice. "There was a hot minute there where we all thought they might, you know, actually be happy together. They were kind of, like, heroes for me and Zoe, when things got a little tough and we hadn't started therapy together yet. We were like, 'One day we're gonna grow up and be like Hailey and Ainsley.'"

Hailey refused to look up from stirring frosting (to accommodate the last-minute request for vegan cake for the half-dozen guests who'd forgotten to fill out their dietary preferences on the RSVP letter); Hailey and Ainsley both knew the "hot minute" Lila meant, and as it had happened on this land, the spirits did, as well. The grand opening of their food truck had been on this very field, surrounded by what Ainsley had dubbed "big gay love," the two working in perfect tandem, Ainsley's eccentric flavor fusions carried out by Hailey's dexterous hand and chemist's eye for spice proportions. None of Hailey's resentment for Ainsley carrying her "kitchen dom energy" into the bedroom had yet emerged, nor Ainsley's exasperation at Hailey's tendency to stew for weeks on end without saying what was on her mind. The two had executed orders swiftly and flawlessly, pausing to peck one another on the cheek to the admiring eyes of their patrons and the suspicious gazes of the spirits of the air and land. The latter, of course, had recognized a performance when they'd seen one; enough generations of tenants had rotted in front of the television on this land that the spirits had seen their share of sitcoms.

Now, on Zoe and Lila's wedding day, the spirits of the flame could feel Hailey burn with the weight of Ainsley's gaze behind her, both women screaming silently into the void, *What happened to us? How did we fall so far?*

The *pièce de résistance* on the spirits' part, however, came when the growing shadows and dwindling guests indicated to Hailey and Ainsley, who hardly spoke to one another at this point in anything beyond single-word grumbles, that they could collect their buffet trays and bow out.

They had parked their food truck far enough from the tent that they could easily pull out. But heat exhaustion and the gathering dark—thickened immensely by the mouse-like spirits of the shadows—ensured that they missed one important detail. As they backed up to turn their truck toward the gravel road, it began to slide backwards faster, and even when Ainsley realized what was happening and shifted to drive, the spirits of the mud pulled with all their strength, and the spirits of the water added moisture from the readily nearby water table to make the ground all the more slippery, and the truck plopped itself firmly into the ditch, which had deepened over the weeks thanks to the spirits of the water and the mud and the clouds. The soft ground cushioned the impact, of course; the spirits did not aim to *harm* Hailey and Ainsley. Quite the opposite!

Guests gathered. Drunk men explained to Hailey and Ainsley that if they turned the steering wheel just this far over and hit the gas just so, while John-Mark and Pauly G. pushed just hard enough, they'd be on their way. Nothing worked. The aforementioned distant cousins stripped off their shoes and rolled up their suit pants, pushing and pushing. The shadows turned to total darkness, and the only light came from the tent's string lights and the fire pits, where dancing or lounging guests pretended not to notice the calamity that had befallen the hired help or convinced themselves that the small crowd around the truck "had it covered."

Ainsley called a tow truck. The concerned guests petered off. The drunk men lost interest, but not without each of them offering Hailey his own inconsistently detailed, well-intended, but ultimately unsolicited suggestion for how Hailey—the more butch of the two and so, in their eyes, presumably the more competent—might avoid this sort of predicament in the future. The spirits smiled among themselves.

That is, until Hailey and Ainsley, in spite of it all, found themselves waiting for the tow truck on an empty couch damp with dew, beside a fire pit whose one wavering ember snuffed out the moment they sat before it, and they curled into the familiar warmth of one another's arms more out of habit than affection. They said nothing. They didn't need to. Nobody understood what tribulations each had been through that evening better than the other. No guest occupied any of the other couches around that particular fire pit nor attempted to revive its flame. None dared.

The spirits of the air and the land and the mud and the shadows and the sky and the stars looked sadly at the neighboring fire, where the newlyweds shared whiskey and stories with their inner circle of remaining friends, then back at Hailey and Ainsley, curled together on their lone couch waiting for the tow truck, apparently closer than ever, in spite of all the signs of doom the spirits had worked so hard to orchestrate.

Well, the spirits had hoped not to spoil the newlyweds' night, but it had to be done. Plump clouds had gathered in case of this very emergency, and perhaps the married couple, at least, would see it as a happy omen. The spirits of the air and the land and the mud and the shadows and the sky and the stars nodded in a symphony of silent agreement, turning their full attention to Hailey and Ainsley.

It began to rain.

RAVENOUS

by Virginia Black

KÖNIGSBERG, PRUSSIA
AUTUMN 1697

"YOU'RE PRESSIN' YOUR LEGENDARY LUCK with this one, Vago." The squat and portly carriage driver spat at the cobblestone and shook his half-bald head in disbelief.

The driver was not the first person to misjudge the likelihood of Elizaveta's fortune, nor would he be the last. His familiarity, however, was a separate issue. Elizaveta adjusted the cravat at her neck hiding her lack of a visible Adam's apple and tugged her gloves into place.

"Come again?" Perhaps a harsh tone would remind him of his place in their arrangement. Two years of employment in her many enterprises did not include the perquisite of informality, not when it might lead to deeper scrutiny.

Such attention must be avoided at all costs.

"My apologies, sir." He tapped the threadbare brim of his cap. "It's just . . . are you sure about this, Mr. Vago?"

"You've been particularly reticent about this endeavor." Most likely, he was superstitious. All common men were. "Why?"

"This place has a reputation—not a good one."

"The contract would pay for the rise you keep suggesting with a distinct lack of subtlety."

The Bartholomew estate was rumored to be the wealthiest in the city with no direct affiliation to the crown, and near legendary consumption of intoxicants. Two hundred cases of wine per annum. One hundred fifty of spirits. Obtaining its contract would triple Elizaveta's yield from all her other customers combined.

Consistent income of that magnitude would provide her wealth enough for a private estate, travel, options for future enterprises—not to mention the privilege of repudiating societal constraints—and would solidify her standing for years to come.

This opportunity was not to be missed.

"We don't really need the business, though, right?" He forced a breath that puffed out his scruffily bearded cheeks. "You just hired two more men for what we got now."

He was a foolish man with no vision, which was why he had to work for her. The referrals from this contract would be invaluable once word spread that she was the manor's sole supplier.

His tone turned wary. "Rumor has it, the servants go missing from here. They only hire people with no family, see. No one to look out for them. My cousin's niece tried to get on here, but she told him all the help looked sickly and barely spoke. Once they heard she had a mum and pa, they sent her away before she—"

Elizaveta cut him off with a raised hand, and then brushed nonexistent dirt from her overcoat. "I am as certain of this venture as you are that the master of the estate is here."

He sighed, defeated, not that he'd stood a chance of convincing her from her path. The advantages of success far outweighed the risks of failure.

"Lem swore his lordship would be here this evening. The master's ship arrived in the harbor with the tide, so he should have been here hours ago. The mistress of the house always hosts a welcome soiree, and after that, Lord Bartholomew retreats, not to be seen again until his next voyage."

He shifted his weight from foot to foot, his twitching an unwelcome distraction when she needed to prepare herself for the work ahead.

"Take the cart back to the warehouse." Luck would no

doubt guide her to other transport back into the heart of the city. Perhaps she was as superstitious as he, but at least her illusions yielded more fruit.

"Invitation only, Mr. Vago. How are you goin' to get in there?"

Elizaveta straightened her shoulders, looming a full head taller than the cart driver, and his pride moved him a step away from her.

"Leave that to me," she said.

He had delivered her onto the estate without detection as directed, and his purpose was fulfilled. She turned her back to him, and the sound of the cartwheels faded behind her as she walked the short path from the side gate to the front of the manor.

Dry, dead leaves crunched under her feet. In the early dark of the autumn evening, the stone path was lit by torches, spaced far enough apart that most of the way lay in shadow. The chill cut through her trousers, but she did not hurry her steps. Only the desperate rushed. Hers was the pace of one confident in what they had accomplished.

Even if the accomplishing was still in progress.

The path led to the manor house where a central three-story hall joined two separate wings, all but a few windows dark. Browned or dead shrubbery framed a courtyard large enough to allow several carriages to wind around a fountain, one bereft of water this late in the season when the frosts might begin any day.

The place where she had been born and raised—a hamlet so tiny, it had no name beyond "that place at the end of the stream"—would have fit entirely in this courtyard. She'd escaped the confinement of her origins a decade ago, and having since created a life beyond such abject poverty, she rarely thought of it.

How strange to be reminded now.

Two guards stood at the bottom of the stairs to the manor's entrance. As she approached, a horse reared nearby, and three men began to argue while another attempted to calm the animal. When another horse spooked, the guards joined the fray, leaving the entrance unattended.

Elizaveta took advantage of the opportunity.

No doorman stood between her and the foyer. Inside the manor, the only activity was the low murmur leading her to the ballroom.

A few familiar faces did not favor her arrival. Two dozen men, including more than one of her competitors, mingled with false camaraderie as if they were not all professionally at each other's throats. Wine or spirits in hand, they all awaited the manor's master.

Yet despite the convivial nature the event might suggest, an undercurrent of discomfort tainted the air. As Elizaveta walked the periphery of the ballroom, one man told a tale with forced humor, his manner and tone not matching his words. Another man laughed too hard, his face red with nerves and his brow slick with sweat.

At the opposite end of the ballroom was an entryway to a dining room devoid of any hint of an evening meal customary at functions similar to this one. Such a deviation from the norm was an example of the eccentricity excused by wealth.

Servants entered and disappeared through two inset doors framed by black velvet curtains, leaving a similar one empty and unattended. All the other attendees had positioned themselves near the entrance they had passed through, expecting the lord of the manor to do the same.

The unmanned entry appeared to be a more likely door through which the lord of the manor might appear. Elizaveta positioned herself beside it, pretending to peruse the furnishings.

Her subterfuge required more effort than usual. Only one painting adorned the largest wall, so washed out and aged the detail required squinting. A hut on a bluff above a tumultuous green sea. Other than that, there was nothing to capture the eye. No family portraits, no coats of arms, no heirlooms, no flowers.

Another revelation—no music filled the silences. Most events of this kind Elizaveta had attended in the past included some accompaniment to aid in the practice of socializing. Here there was only the tense conversation of nervous people—

otherwise, the ballroom was surprisingly empty.

A man matching her height approached with a silver tray covered in champagne flutes, his eyes blank and his face motionless. She wanted no glass of wine or spirit. Keeping her wits about her would lift her above this common crowd, setting her apart from the glad-handers, the obsequious, and the overly presumptuous.

She declined his offer, and he slithered back into the crowd. The servants had either been trained well or punished thoroughly—perhaps both.

"The good and fortunate Mr. Benedek Vago," said a mellifluous voice from the nebulous shadows of the black curtains behind her. "I don't recall seeing your name on the invitation list."

The shadows resolved into a comely woman of slight stature, no taller than Elizaveta's shoulder. The woman's accusation sounded more entertained than offended. Perhaps she wouldn't show Elizaveta the door.

She seemed familiar enough with Elizaveta's assumed name and had entered from the hidden corners of the house. A resident, then, one who might have Lord Bartholomew's ear.

Charm was not Elizaveta's strongest suit, but forthrightness was.

"My apologies for my impulsivity, madame, but such an event was not to be missed." She bowed in deference. "Do I have the pleasure of meeting Lady Bartholomew?"

The woman's face was symmetrical, her nose aquiline but flattering. Her hair was pale, as white as her skin, which looked as if she had not spent any time in the sun recently. She was thin and slightly built and dressed in a black gown of exquisite and rare fabric, with a silken wrap over her shoulders. She appeared almost sickly, yet her demeanor was spirited and in good humor, as if Elizaveta's arrival—Benedek's arrival—was a welcome surprise.

"I am not, though I do act as the lady of the manor. Lord Bartholomew is not married."

Perhaps she was his mistress. If so, their arrangement might be considered sordid by societal standards, though they might not care. Another example of wealth's ignored improprieties.

"I've heard some mention of your ventures, Mr. Vago, but little about you, so tell me." She tilted her head forward and glanced through her lashes as she smiled. "Were you born in this fair city?"

Habitual reticence spoke for Elizaveta, stunned as she was by this woman's appearance and by her own curiosity about the woman's identity. "No, I was born in the north."

She never shared any personal details about herself and must be careful to reveal nothing this evening.

The woman persisted. "And do you have family here?"

"No, madame."

Elizaveta's father, a stonecutter, had died when she was a child, followed by her mother a few years later from grief, overwork, and disappointment. The latter she had blamed on her children.

Benedek, Elizaveta's younger brother by a year, had been a shiftless drunk who wasted any available coin at the pub in a town over the hills from their hovel. He had viewed his sister as nothing but a bride price and had been constantly displeased with her lack of prospects.

One winter morning, she'd cut his cold, dead corpse from their mule. Someone had been kind enough to tie him to the animal, assuming it would carry Benedek's unconscious body home. Her brother had frozen to death overnight.

Their resemblance had long been touted as an unfortunate circumstance. Elizaveta thought otherwise and found his name more valuable in his passing.

She was reminded of the cart driver's warnings about the servants of the manor having no family but cast them aside.

"I found the city teeming with opportunities to serve," Elizaveta said, "and endeavor to meet them."

The woman laughed, a brittle yet provocative sound.

"So you're not one of Lord Bartholomew's many . . .

admirers?" She glanced in the direction of the gathered assembly.

A few of the men were daring in their presentation before Lord Bartholomew, effusive in their praise, almost . . . flirtatious. Perhaps they were less interested in becoming one of the master's vendors than in chasing a position in his bed.

"I daresay I am not." Elizaveta must be careful not to offend. "Though I do commend his many philanthropic efforts."

Not that she knew of any, but wealthy men like him always tithed to some sort of public work or charity, the better to impress their benevolence upon lesser folk.

The woman's eyes widened in astonishment. Her irises were perhaps the palest blue or gray, their outlines a stark red—a probable trick of the light cast by the chandelier. The whites of her eyes appeared bloodshot, as if she'd not slept well of late.

She smiled as if Elizaveta had presented her with a gift.

"How could anyone mistake you for a man?" Her voice was little more than a whisper.

Elizaveta's fear of exposure and condemnation stole her breath. Many—everyone—had believed her deception and taken her presentation and demeanor as truth. Once she'd abandoned her family's home and escaped to a distant village, assuming her brother's name had been as simple as donning male attire and affecting the mannerisms of men. Her features had been deemed plain enough to suit her chosen identity.

Then again, no one had stood this close to her in a long time. She may have been too shocked to deny the accusation, but habit kept her still as the woman laughed.

"What a quandary you've made for yourself." The woman wiped away tears of delight. "You don't want anyone to look too closely, but, oh, you want to be seen, don't you?"

Years of self-preservation might have pushed Elizaveta a step back, but the attraction of being recognized and not abhorred pulled her forward. The woman clasped her arm as if they were old friends, her smile warm and her manner welcoming.

"Oh, I won't reveal your secret," the woman said, amusement curling her lips as she leaned closer. When she smiled, she revealed near perfect teeth, though two of them were oddly pointed. "You are far too sensational and lovely a find to let common ignorance steal you away. Most people are simple fools who can't see the beauty in those who are truly exceptional."

In Elizaveta's entire life, no one had ever mentioned beauty in reference to her person.

Though the woman's cheek did not touch Elizaveta's, the proximity of her skin was a brazen caress.

"I see you quite well," she said, her voice low and suggestive in a way Elizaveta had heard directed at others in the shadowed corners of parlor rooms, but never herself. The woman stood so close her captivating perfume filled the air. To be near enough to enjoy it seemed inappropriate, almost base, almost . . .

Carnal. A hint at sensual delights Elizaveta had never shared with another.

Her hands twitched at her sides, and her fingers felt swollen in her gloves. She ached to remove them, but such impolite informality might suggest the possibility of other indiscretions.

A rising murmur drew Elizaveta's attention toward the other entrance. Lord Bartholomew marched into the ballroom, and the air in the room changed with his arrival. He was not tall, nor was he exceptionally attractive or jovial, but he held the focus of every other man in the room. He greeted them with detached civility, unsmiling but polite.

Elizaveta's luck hadn't guided her to him. She had misjudged and lost any chance at an advantage. While the woman at her side was compelling—entertaining even, assuming she kept Elizaveta's true nature a secret as she pledged to do—she was not the reason Elizaveta had gone to all the trouble of attending.

The woman in question leaned forward, her pale décolletage capturing the light. "Now I shall tell you a secret, and we shall build a confidence between us, yes? The man before you is not the master of this house."

No rumor Elizaveta had gleaned in her extensive research had hinted at such a truth. If he was some charlatan, if this was a hoax—

"Oh, it is all his, of course," the woman said with a sigh. "The manor, the many enterprises, the ships. But he is far too distracted to pay it much mind. May I grow so old yet pay better interest in the world around me."

Some judgment was hidden in her tone, but Elizaveta was preoccupied. Something about the way the others approached Lord Bartholomew hinted at details she felt a pull to determine.

Though the men across the room circled Lord Bartholomew, none of them offered to shake his hand in greeting. None stood close enough to touch him at all. They kept their distance, bowing and offering solicitations.

One man, so overweight he taxed the buttons on his coat, doffed his hat and bowed. The hat shook in his trembling hands.

They appeared desperate for Lord Bartholomew's recognition, but not enough to get too close to him. Almost as if they were afraid of him.

"Believe me, Mister Vago," the woman said, whispering into Elizaveta's ear. "Pursuing his attention is a waste of your good time. If you've some sort of proposition you wish to offer, nothing comes into this manor unless I will it. You should be wooing my approval."

A ghost of a kiss brushed Elizaveta's cheek in brazen and clear invitation.

Elizaveta glanced at Lord Bartholomew, whose attention was focused on a young man who fawned and stuttered while the others jockeyed for conversational position. She pondered the intriguing puzzle before her.

Leaving the ballroom and sacrificing such an opportunity on the word of a stranger would be folly.

The woman slid her hand inside Elizaveta's coat and pressed against her side. When she tilted her head as if to suggest Elizaveta had only a moment to decide, Elizaveta chose to leave Lord Bartholomew to his fawning audience.

With a tug at her sleeve, the woman drew Elizaveta through the velvet curtains and the hidden door into a cool, dimly lit hall, empty of servants or guests. The rest of their conversation was not verbal.

Something akin to wonder, like joy, spread through Elizaveta's chest at their first true kiss. An ache in her limbs, in her body, at her center, exiled good sense as she followed the woman down the dark halls. She only had time to notice the furnishings here were as sparse as the ballroom, and all the surfaces were pristine and devoid of dust, but a faint odor of mildew or rot emanated from the corners.

They startled one servant, who evidently expected no one. The lady said nothing, but the girl looked horrified and quickly disappeared. The servant's parting glance seemed to impart some indecipherable message to Elizaveta, who was promptly distracted by another heart-racing kiss.

The bedroom contained only a bed—no chest of drawers, no privy, no station for libations or other refreshments—but she had no time to consider the oddity before the lady pried at Elizaveta's clothes.

For the first time, she stood naked before another human being, who looked back at her as if she were the most desirable person in creation before pulling her into bed.

Elizaveta had prepared herself to suffer the idiosyncrasies of the wealthy this night—the demands to provide some favor or rare trinket in trade for a contract. Once, a potential client had avidly solicited Elizaveta to marry his daughter. How horrified he might have been to suggest such a thing had he known her true nature.

This was hardly a price at all, though before they committed to a deeper union, she ought to obtain one additional piece of information.

"Your name, madame."

The woman who would be her lover laughed.

"You may call me Hannelore, my pet. And yours? Your true name, I mean." She bit Elizaveta's lower lip, those strange teeth nipping at her flesh.

"I . . . my . . ." Words failed as Elizaveta stared at the trace of blood on Hannelore's lips.

Hannelore arched a pale eyebrow, a wicked glint sparkling in her eyes.

"Tell me later," she said, and pulled Elizaveta closer to claim her kiss.

The few hours spent in Hannelore's bed—in her arms—taught Elizaveta more about her own body than all the years before. She had held herself confidently as she moved through the world. She passed as a man, yes, but she did not deny the truth of the woman inside her manly vestments.

Yet now, she found much of herself had been undiscovered—so many sensations she didn't know her body was capable of. Hannelore's attention was unflagging, her affection and admiration seemingly sincere, and each apex of rapture was soon overshadowed by the next.

Whatever they were doing—and Elizaveta had no names for most of their actions—had to be sinful, not that she wanted to stop.

Educated by Hannelore's example, Elizaveta sought to lift her new lover to the same heights. As the hours passed, she hoped this night would not be her only opportunity to share such pleasure with this singular woman.

From intrigued to besotted in one evening. She almost disregarded her original intent in coming to the manor, though she wouldn't be so tasteless as to bring it up now. Not when she had other, far more intriguing things holding her interest.

Captivated by her lover's gaze, Elizaveta pushed herself down the bed for her next attempt at a demonstrated act, kicking the linens aside as Hannelore laughed. The delectable—no, mouthwatering redolence at the join of Hannelore's torso and thigh . . . all the worship paid in many a church pew had not been as devout as her reverence now.

She slowed, eager to savor the moment.

New feelings paired with senses heightened by the

experience. Her own ragged breath filled her ears, as well as Hannelore's sighs, but so did the rush of her own blood in her veins, the whisper of skin against skin and every susurrus murmur of the shifting bed linens.

The fire. The fire was another presence in the room. Without glancing at the hearth, she knew how wide the fire stretched, how high the flames rose before transforming into smoke. She knew how many candles were lit in the room. Her mother—not a witch, but near enough to one to possess some skill with herbs and hexes—had always said Elizaveta had an affinity for the flame.

She'd also said Elizaveta was cursed with bad luck, but the present situation suggested otherwise.

Still, there was something else, something at the edge of her understanding, tingling in her fingertips—

"It's intoxicating, isn't it?" Hannelore asked after voicing the peak of her pleasure. She pushed Elizaveta onto her back and slid over her, a hidden strength in her smaller limbs. With a gentle, knowing smile, she traced Elizaveta's lips with the tip of her finger, and Elizaveta shivered at the touch.

"Can you feel the new power racing through your veins?" Hannelore asked.

What power?

Hannelore leaned forward, her tongue following the path of her finger. Her perfume filled Elizaveta's sharpened senses, overpowering the thick nutty aroma of the crackling fire. That floral scent again, a rare flower perhaps, with a hint of something unpleasant.

Something rancid or decayed.

Something dead.

"Oh, you sweet, handsome creature." Hannelore pressed one hand at Elizaveta's throat, pushing her down, holding her captive. "I thought I might take my fill and be done, but . . . you are far too precious to waste."

She licked and nipped at Elizaveta's earlobe before kissing below her ear.

And then Hannelore bit Elizaveta's neck with her strange teeth. At first, Elizaveta quickened at this new, dangerous touch, perhaps the beginning of a new blissful lesson.

Desire became discomfort, became pain.

"Hannelore—"

An animalistic moan accompanied a thick, swallowing sound, wiping away any trace of Elizaveta's ardor. Horror spread through her like the icy bite of winter's cold.

Hannelore was consuming her blood.

Elizaveta pushed against Hannelore's shoulders, accomplishing nothing with the effort.

Hannelore pinioned Elizaveta against the pillows that had so recently been their lover's nest, confining her with inhuman strength.

Elizaveta could not move, and then she could not scream.

———

Whispers pulled Elizaveta awake. Someone was speaking to her. A soft voice, one that brought an accompanying tendril of fear.

". . . so alone all these years," the voice said. "But now . . . I will show you so much, pet, in the world beyond this trivial place. Even Bartholomew will agree."

The stench of blood and urine and excrement, of offal and disuse, of her own unwashed body assailed Elizaveta's senses.

She opened her eyes. She sat half upright, naked and uncovered in an uncomfortable chair, her arms strapped in place. Objects she couldn't identify or interpret poked into her veins.

Hannelore stood beside her, clad in only her nightdress, streams of blood on her chin. Across the room, two women sat sleeping, propped against the wall and each other, their necks dark with dried blood.

No. They weren't asleep—their eyes were open and dead.

Hannelore traced her fingers over Elizaveta's brow. "What pleasures I will show you, now that we have all the time in the world."

A foreign panic filled Elizaveta. No chill or tremor moved her, no perspiration rose on her skin. Her body did not feel like her own. She wasn't tired; she was exhausted. She wasn't thirsty; she was dying for something wet, something more than water. The craving wracked her.

Strange urges swept through her limbs that she couldn't define, but Hannelore was the cause.

"What have you done to me?"

Hannelore smiled as if she had granted Elizaveta an impossible desire. "I have made you like me, dear heart."

"Like you?" Sickly? Strange and somewhat unhinged? Perverse and depraved? None of that was contagious or could be passed from person to person in so short a time.

How long had she been here?

Hannelore's smile did not fade, though her odd eyes were sad. "For so long—years, and more than I can count—I have lived in Bartholomew's wake. We are companions of a kind, though not lovers. These last few years, we've barely been friends. He mourns those long lost times forever past."

She frowned, a bitterness seeping into her voice.

"He has become boring. I cannot bear him alone any longer, but now you've come. You said you'd found opportunities here, to serve." She kissed Elizaveta's brow. "Now you can serve me, and the ways I will reward you will make those hours we shared seem tame."

Elizaveta had served her mother and her brother, enduring their subjugation and denigration until their deaths. Serving a madwoman, no matter how enamored Elizaveta might be, was the last thing she wanted. What were the chances an arrangement with Hannelore would yield anything different when Elizaveta's own wants and desires had not been considered?

She tugged at the bindings, and they fell away, the objects clanking on the chair and the floor. Blood dripped from her arms, and she dared to peer again at the still corpses across the room.

"What happened to them?" Elizaveta pointed at the dead bodies. "Did . . . did you kill them?"

"Shh . . . of course I did." Hannelore's smile was as tender as it had been in her bed. "I needed them to sustain me while I helped you."

"Helped me?" Horror swelled in Elizaveta's chest, tainted with sorrow that she had had some part in their demise.

"They don't matter, my sweet. We'll feed from a thousand like them—"

Without thought, Elizaveta clamped her hand over Hannelore's now stammering mouth, willing her silent. Rage, fear, confusion—a maelstrom swirled inside her.

The life she had imagined for herself evaporated. She was now privy to murder, with nothing to protect her from its penalties, from the resulting exposure of her person. She could not be trapped again, imprisoned in truth or by someone else's ideal of whom she should be, how she should live.

Whom she should serve.

Hannelore struggled, but Elizaveta rose from the chair and shoved Hannelore into her place. She did not let her rise, did not release her hand. Hannelore's eyes widened as her feeble attempts to escape proved fruitless.

What could be done? Elizaveta did not even know where she was, though she imagined she was somewhere in the manor. And where was Lord Bartholomew? Did he know such things occurred in his house? What if he was aware and complacent?

Something was burning—something acrid and foul. Elizaveta's hand was glowing. Hannelore's muffled screams tapered into a croak, and the skin around Elizaveta's fingers turned red, and then orange, and then black.

Hannelore stopped moving. Her eyes had become somehow desiccated in their sockets. Elizaveta lifted her hand, and cried out at the burned and twisted flesh beneath it.

This dreadful and beautiful creature who had brought such joy, such light, such bonding emotion—and such unconscionable and irrevocable damage—was dead.

Elizaveta's crying out became a keening.

What had she done? How in creation had she done it?

The painful craving seized Elizaveta again, and she fought against it until reason returned.

More than one person had seen her at the ball. One of the servants had seen her on the way to Hannelore's rooms. It would not take long for Lord Bartholomew and the authorities to determine who might be responsible. Even if she could plead some sort of defense under the circumstances, her identity would be revealed.

No matter what happened next, she could not stay here.

The horrid room with its grisly contents was on the first floor, and Elizaveta ran toward the light through the windows until she found a door leading outside.

The first frost crunched beneath her naked feet as she fled toward the woods bordering the manor.

She put her faith in luck one more time.

Two nights later the moon rose over the water on the horizon. Elizaveta stood near the bow of a three-masted ship, clenching her gloved hands against the railing.

The gloves kept her from inadvertently setting fire to her surroundings.

The crew avoided her, sensing her strangeness. Though once again dressed as a man, she felt a difference in the way she carried herself, a foreign power and weight to her limbs.

If what she feared was true, the crew was right in thinking themselves in danger. She was now a predator, one whose nature she could not fathom. In time, and though the thought repulsed her, she would have to feed on the crew to survive.

She would prevail, no matter how horrid her life had become. She had not come this far to surrender to circumstance now.

A whisper of fabric was her only warning.

"Surely you could have found easier ways to escape pursuit," a voice said beside her.

Her new reflexes kept her from flinching. An unfamiliar

sensation passed like a wave through her body, one no longer bound by mere human limitations. Perhaps it was the urge to fight or flee, though she wasn't sure which she wanted more.

Lord Bartholomew stood beyond arm's reach, his hands loosely clasped behind his back. He had left his more formal and stately vestments behind and stood in a tunic and pants, without an overcoat despite the night's chill. The clothes appeared damp, yet no fog thickened the air.

Two nights ago, he had been dressed like a wealthy elitist. Now he looked like a simple tradesman, and he appeared weary, not in form but in bearing. To her amazement, she stood taller than he, though it likely gave her no advantage.

If he was here to kill her, she was not certain what fight she might provide to defend herself.

How had he boarded this ship without her knowledge?

He turned his head, and Elizaveta forced herself not to leap overboard. His eyes were white, with barely a tint to the line separating the iris from the sclera. Whoever—whatever—he was, he was something far different from Hannelore. Elizaveta wondered how quickly or violently her death would come.

"Why America?" he asked, revealing his knowledge of her destination. His tenor voice was calm, but carried a hint of menace, and his expression demanded an answer.

Parched—perhaps from the salt in the air, perhaps from her new thirst for the hot viscosity of human blood—she found speech difficult.

"To find somewhere to begin anew," she said without equivocation. What good would lying do her now?

"Not just to flee, then?"

Escape was her first inclination, but there was something else. Some need twitching beyond her understanding that had nothing to do with her murderous wake, or her quest for wealth, or even—if she could bring herself to admit it—her taste for blood.

"You are far from boring, aren't you?" He did not seem angry—he was curious, or perhaps amused, as if she were a conundrum to be solved.

Elizaveta did not move.

"Perhaps I too will try something new," he said, a weariness bleeding into his tone. "I have lived a long time, longer than you can imagine, longer than the countries you are leaving behind have existed. I was old when ships such as this one were first invented."

He leaned forward, bracing himself against the railing as if he could no longer hold himself upright. Elizaveta suspected, at the sight of talons where his fingernails might be, that he was much stronger than he appeared.

He pressed his lips in a line before speaking again. "Hannelore was not mine, but I felt some . . . responsibility for her. I will not punish or censure you for her death. We are a volatile kind, and I doubt you were aware of your own powers."

He glanced at her gloves. Did he know what she was now capable of? What kind were they? Who was she now?

"More than once," he continued, "the newly turned have rebelled against their sires. Those first few moments are difficult, and the shock itself can be a trial. You seem to have kept your wits about you, which is commendable."

He tilted his head forward, and the moonlight drowned in his milky eyes. "But you will not escape my governance. I will not confine or detain you, and I will not demand your service, but I cannot leave you to wander the world unattended."

Her terror ebbed for a moment at the thought of being tended to like a child, though she said nothing.

The corner of his mouth turned, not a smile but not displeasure either. "I see your pride already balks at such restraints, and believe me, I have no interest in taking on another charge. I will accompany you on your travels and we shall see what this new land might offer those such as us, but I will have two things from you before then."

He turned toward her again, his stance brooking no dissembling or argument. Not that Elizaveta planned to protest. She sensed his strength, his power, though he did nothing to impress her with it.

"First, your true name."

"Elizaveta Vago," she said, a deep-seated relief overtaking her, despite her current danger.

After a long moment he nodded. "Second, an honest answer to this one question. Is there anything you value more than your ambition?"

He had seen her in the room with the others, with only one reason for any of those men and herself to be present. They had sought the master's favor.

She had captured it, though not how she had hoped.

"My freedom," she said, surprising herself with her candor.

Bartholomew's brow was furrowed as he considered her answer. He stood for some time and said nothing more.

Assured she would not die this night, Elizaveta returned her gaze to the moonlit sea.

IN SPEARY WOOD

A Prequel to *The Demon Equilibrium*

---

by Cathy Pegau

CHARLESBURG, OHIO, 1871

"WHERE COULD HE BE?" Tommie Caldwell asked herself for the umpteenth time. Her brother James had failed to return as expected earlier that afternoon and she was less than pleased. "A simple delivery. That's all he had to do."

As they traveled Speary Wood Road, Old Gert the mule gave her usual response: a whinny that ended in a worried grumble.

Tommie could relate. She'd had to close the store early to come all the way out here to Speary Wood, half fearful she'd find James hurt along the way and half angry that he had gone off fishing with his friends. Her stomach knotted with either possibility.

But he wouldn't have taken Barney and the cart fishing. At fifteen, James was impetuous at times, but not irresponsible, especially when it came to proper care of their animals and belongings.

Since Mam and Da had passed, leaving only the two of them, they'd both had to grow up quick. The family store was doing well enough, and Tommie was proud of what they'd managed together. In a few years, she'd feel comfortable enough to find someone to settle down with and leave James to run things.

If she didn't kill him first.

Tommie urged Gert off the dirt road that bisected Speary

Wood and onto the weedy two-track that led to the Palmer place. Gert plodded along, dappled late afternoon sunlight coming through the trees, emphasizing her graying muzzle and ears. She wasn't a fast ride, but better than Tommie walking the three miles herself. Besides, Gert enjoyed getting out in the sunshine. There should be plenty of light left of the summer day if they could get James and turn right around and go back home.

Less than a hundred yards from Speary Wood Road, the trees grew together overhead, closing out much of that sunlight, taking its heat away. Tommie shivered in the sudden coolness. Nothing stirred in the Wood. Not a squirrel, not a bird. The only sound was Gert's hooves on the packed path.

They came to the wooden bridge that crossed the creek, and Gert stopped without Tommie having to touch the reins. On the other side, the windows of the neat, humble home—a cabin, really—glowed softly. Not the sort of place she'd imagined a gruff man like Virgil Palmer to live. She'd expected ramshackle and rough, not curtains and tidy flower boxes.

Like everyone in town, she'd heard the rumors about Mr. Palmer, about how he'd once killed a man for looking at his wife, how he'd shrunk into himself after Mrs. Palmer had died. He came to the store regularly to conduct his business, then left without chatting like other customers tended to do. Not exactly friendly, but not frightening or intimidating. Still, when Tommie and James found a list of goods and some money shoved under the store's door along with a note requesting delivery due to illness, they'd reluctantly agreed it was the neighborly thing to do.

Had James run into trouble? Was Mr. Palmer too sick to leave alone?

Tommie slid off Gert and took hold of her reins to guide the mule over the bridge. Gert whimpered and refused to budge.

"Come on," Tommie whispered. "I'm not sure—"

I'm not sure you're safe out here alone.

Where had that come from? There was no danger from the Wood; predators weren't known to frequent this particular area.

Rather than fight with Gert—a losing battle for everyone—

Tommie loosely tied Gert's reins around a low tree branch. She'd stay put unless something really scared her; then she'd at least be able to get away.

Away from what?

Tommie crossed the bridge, eyes on the cabin, ears perked. Still nothing. But *something* set her on edge. Staying in the shadows, she walked the perimeter of the clearing, around the cabin. A yard with a three-rail fence sectioned off an area behind the home and small barn, though Mr. Palmer's horse and two goats weren't visible.

The entire property felt abandoned, except for the light within.

Where was James? Barney and the cart? Had they even made it to Palmer's place? She would have passed them on the road, or seen some sign of trouble.

Tommie approached the front door, her stomach tight and her hands growing warm. She wiped her palms on her skirts, then raised a fist to knock. The door swung open before she could connect.

A young blonde woman, not much older than Tommie's own eighteen years, stood with one hand on the latch and the other holding a large knife. Her summer green dress brushed the tops of her bare feet.

"Who have we here?"

"Good afternoon. My name is Tommie Caldwell. From the general store. Mr. Palmer had us deliver some goods. Is James here? He was supposed to return hours ago. We need him home."

I need him home. There was no "we" anymore.

"Of course. Why don't you come in? I'm Eliza."

"Eliza?"

"Yes, Eliza Palmer. Virgil Palmer is my father."

Virgil Palmer had a daughter? Tommie had never heard of her, and in a small town everyone knew everyone. But Tommie's family was new to the area, having arrived a decade ago from Scotland. They weren't necessarily privy to local genealogy, especially when it came to a recluse like Mr. Palmer. Perhaps this daughter had lived elsewhere for some reason. That had to be it. Otherwise, Tommie surely would have met her at some point.

Eliza turned away and crossed the cozy front room to a table with piles of vegetables. The room was overly warm, the fire roaring beneath a covered black iron pot on a swinging hook sunk into the brick hearth.

"I don't mean to interrupt your supper. I just want to collect James."

"No interruption. Come in, come in."

Everything in Tommie's being told her to get away from Eliza Palmer. Every bone in her body and hair standing on her nape said, "Run!" But she couldn't. Wouldn't. James was here, or had been, and she wasn't leaving without him.

"Please," she said stepping into the room, leaving the door open. "I just want to get James and go home."

Never had she meant words more sincerely.

"I'm sure James is around here somewhere," Eliza said, an infernally bright grin on her face as she chopped vegetables.

"Somewhere?"

"He offered to help look for one of the goats that escaped. Went out with the—my father." She gestured toward the two chairs nearest the table. "Please. Sit."

The skin on the nape of Tommie's neck tingled uncomfortably as she lowered herself onto the chair farthest from Eliza.

"The note left at the store said your father was ill."

"He's feeling better."

"If James is helping him, where are our horse and cart?"

Eliza chopped an onion into irregular pieces, as if she didn't know or care to make them more uniform. "Out back. The horse needed water."

Tommie frowned. Neither horse nor cart were in the back when she'd circled the property. Could they have been in the barn? Why? Why tell such a blatant lie?

"They're not there, Miss Palmer. And I didn't see any sign of him on the road."

"No? Perhaps James returned without stopping in, then

went off somewhere. Not very polite of him." Another onion met the knife with a dull *thud*.

"He wouldn't do that."

He might. No, not take the entire afternoon knowing Tommie would worry. "And your father isn't back either?"

Eliza shrugged. "Not that I've seen, but then again, we aren't keen on keeping so close an eye on one another." She met Tommie's eyes and tilted her head, smiling. "Not like you and your brother."

"I should go find him. Thank you for your help."

Such as it was.

Tommie rose and backed toward the door. Keeping the other woman in sight seemed prudent. Eliza nodded once, and the door slammed shut. Tommie jumped out of her skin, whirling toward the door, half expecting someone to be standing there, having come in. But there was no one.

She turned back to Eliza, heart pounding, hands sweating. The smile on the woman's face was a wide rictus. Her eyes shone with a malevolence that Tommie felt in her bones like a bruise.

"Sit down," Eliza growled.

Tommie started to comply with the command, but something stopped her. Something building up from the pit of her stomach, spreading toward her spine and limbs, made her say, "No."

Eliza's slender eyebrows rose. Tommie watched Eliza's hand gripping a raw potato. Her fingers flexed. The white flesh of the tuber and the dirt brown skin were pulverized to mush with a soft crunch.

No normal woman was that strong.

Tommie quivered as if she'd stepped out into a bitterly cold night, but she wasn't cold. She felt feverish and, scared as she was, anger swirled with the fear.

"Where's James?"

"I'd be more concerned about my own self if I were you, girl."

Eliza threw the knife at her.

The air around Tommie crackled like lightning. She held her crossed arms up to deflect the blade—better a cut there than in the chest. Her body warmed like a sudden fever had taken her. The knife stopped dead, hovering before her eyes as if held by an invisible savior. She blinked. It clattered to the floor.

Tommie met Eliza's wide-eyed gaze with her own. "God a'mighty."

Eliza grinned. "Oh, this'll be fun."

She came around the table and swung her arm, palm out. Tommie's head snapped sideways, her cheek stinging from the slap that never physically connected.

In her head, she knew what Eliza was doing was impossible, yet it was happening. And if Tommie didn't do something, she would be dead.

Dead like James.

No. No no no. She shook off the very idea.

Heart racing, Tommie snatched up the knife at her feet and pointed it at Eliza. "Stay away from me."

Eliza raised her clawlike hand, fingers bent, nails now an inch long, sharp, and black. She came at Tommie. Before Eliza could strike, Tommie thrust the knife up under her ribs. She felt the blade sink to the hilt into Eliza's body.

Black blood trickled from Eliza's grinning mouth. "Nice hit, but it's not silver."

"What . . ."

Eliza grabbed Tommie by the throat, lifted her off her feet, and shoved her against the wall. Tommie's head bounced against the plaster-covered lath. She clawed at the hand, scraping flesh with her nails. Stifled breath burned in her chest. Her eyes throbbed.

Eliza pulled the knife from her chest and tossed it aside. Blackness oozed out of the wound, staining the pale green dress. Her red and black tongue flicked across her lips.

That can't be. The knock to my head has me seeing things.

"You will be particularly delicious." Eliza leaned in and trailed her tongue along Tommie's cheek. It felt like a coarser version of a cat's tongue, yet slimy like a snail.

Tommie shuddered, her gorge rising as far as her clenched throat. Her eyes watered at the acidic sting.

The thing called Eliza laughed and swung Tommie around, setting her down on the ladder-back chair with a force that jolted her spine.

"Sit. And don't move." Eliza released her.

Tommie gasped air into her deprived lungs. Tears streamed down her cheeks as she took great gulps. Tears of relief, of fear, of anger. She wiped her face with the sleeves of her dress. Falling apart would get her nowhere.

"Now, what sort of games shall we play? Surely someone like yourself can withstand more than the average person." Eliza grinned, black blood staining small, pointed teeth. "More than an old man or a boy, for certain."

Tommie's heart seemed to stop. "What did you do to him?"

Eliza made a concerned face that Tommie knew was insincere and mocking. "You don't want to hear those nasty details, do you?" Her expression brightened. "But I'll tell you. I want to feel your glorious pain and sorrow as I describe what happened right in the very chair you now occupy."

If she could have, Tommie would have bolted from the seat.

She swallowed tears and sniffed back snot. "Why? Why did you hurt him?"

James was a sweet boy beneath all the rough-and-tumble attributes of his age and gender. Never a cross word or ill thought for anyone. What could he have said or done to merit any harm?

"He was here."

It was that simple. This thing—for now Tommie could not look at the sharp-toothed mouth and clawed hands and black blood and consider Eliza human—hurt her James, would hurt her, just for being in the same room.

"And Mr. Palmer?"

Eliza shrugged. "Gone about two weeks now. He was so full of hate and anger, I didn't have to feed for days after. The animals weren't enough to sustain me, so I put in an order at your little store."

The words she spoke were English, yet Tommie couldn't make them make sense in her head. The gist of her actions were clear enough.

"You're a monster."

"I've been called worse by better than you, girl." Eliza leaned a hip against the table and crossed her arms. "We know what I am. The question is, do you know what *you* are?"

Tommie blinked at her. What was Eliza talking about?

"I'm just a girl."

Eliza threw back her head and laughed, her fanged mouth gaping. When she met Tommie's gaze again, her eyes were solid black orbs. "No, you aren't. And the best part is, you don't even realize it. But I like to live dangerously. Let's see what you can do. Get up."

The air around her seemed to shimmer. Tommie found herself able to stand. Eliza crossed the room and turned to face her, a confident, smug smile on her distorted face.

"You're about to understand you have it in you to fight me and will lose anyway, making you much more of a delightful morsel than anything I've had in eons."

She flicked her wrist and a black glob streaked across the room. It hit Tommie in the chest, sending her stumbling backward. Searing pain spread from her chest, along her limbs. She cried out, fell to her knees. Then the pain was gone, leaving her panting on the floor.

"Tsk tsk. Not very quick, are you? Better be prepared, girl. This next one is going to be a doozy."

The Eliza-thing drew her arm back.

Tommie's heart rate jumped. A buzzing sound between her ears was all at once distracting and encouraging. Something was happening, happening to her, but what?

As Eliza threw whatever invisible projectile she was holding, Tommie instinctively raised her hands to shield her face. Bluish light rimmed her spread hands. What was this?

Something hit her hands. Tommie felt the impact, but she wasn't hurt. The light surrounding her skin flared and deepened to indigo. The invisible attack dissipated.

"Ah, see! I knew you had it in you," Eliza crowed. "This is much more entertaining than the easy pickings of an old man or little boy. They both cried, begged. Pathetic. Sad little people leading sad little lives. I did them a favor, actually. Put them out of their misery."

"James wasn't miserable." The words came out in a half sob.

"Wasn't he? He wanted to be treated like an adult, but you always ran roughshod over him, over his ideas. Since your parents died, you weren't his sister anymore. You were his boss. What orphan needs a boss?" She laughed at whatever part of that she considered to be funny.

He thought that? Why hadn't he said anything? She didn't mean to make him unhappy. They'd had so much sadness the past year.

Pain lanced through Tommie's chest and she breathed hard to try to control it. Eliza grinned, knowing her words—her lies—caused more damage than any physical attack.

"But you're a fighter, Tommie. You'll lose, but you'll fight me first. I like that."

She threw a handful of black flame.

Tommie didn't merely deflect it this time. She "caught" the flames, which turned deep blue, and hurled them right back.

Eliza's eyes went wide as the flames engulfed her. She screamed in shocked pain, quickly moving her arms about to extinguish the fire that burned holes in her pretty green dress. Tommie didn't know what she was doing—just going with her gut, as Da would say.

"You bitch! You utterly surprising bitch." Eliza laughed again, then her expression changed. "Playtime is over."

Tommie's stomach churned as she braced herself. "My thoughts exactly."

Eliza whipped her hands forward. Tommie raised her arms to block whatever she threw. It felt like a tree had swung right into her. She flew back, tumbling over the table and hitting the floor. Breath whooshed out of her. The buzzing in her head winked out. The blue of her hands flicked out. She shook her head, clambered to her hands and knees.

A clawed hand clamped around her throat. Needles of pain pierced her. Unable to breathe, she was dragged to her feet. Then she was off the floor.

The Eliza-thing stared at her with those flat black orbs. "You lose, girl."

A voice made itself heard in Tommie's head. Mam's voice. *You are a Caldwell. Act accordingly.*

"So do you," Tommie eked out.

She grasped the thing's forearms and drew upon whatever it was inside her that had helped her earlier. Her vision darkened, then tinged blue. Her body burned, not with fever but with blistering fire that radiated from her.

Eliza screamed in rage and let her go. Her dress and flesh burned. The stench of charring, rotted meat hit Tommie in the face. She gagged as she fell to her knees. Eliza swiped at the blue flames, but the effort only spread the fiery light. Her rage became pain.

Through the roaring in her head, Tommie heard the door bang against the wall.

Eliza snarled and raised a hand as orange and purple balls streaked toward her, adhering to her skin and clothing. The rainbow of flames covered her, burning away the dress, blackening her pale skin.

Tommie peered from beneath the table. Two women in simple clothing, one of African descent and the other appearing to be northern European, took turns throwing fireballs at Eliza. Eliza alternately moved her hands as if throwing her own invisible missiles and holding them up to defend herself, all the while screeching obscenities. The blue flames Tommie had been responsible for petered out. She scurried to the farthest corner she could reach, gulping for breath.

The pale blonde woman stopped briefly and laid her hand on the other's arm. The Black woman seemed to grow taller. Her next attack was a shaft of purple light that formed in her hand.

She threw it. The light spear impaled Eliza's flaming body and carried her back into the wall. Eliza hit with a solid thud that shook the small house. Suspended as she was, Eliza pawed and clawed ineffectually at the pulsing spear.

The Black woman walked over to her. "Be gone from this plane."

She pressed her palm against Eliza's forehead. Eliza's skin smoked, her fanged mouth open in a silent scream. Within moments, her body turned to ash and crumbled to the ground. The purple shaft faded to nothing.

Tommie stared at the blackened mark on the wall. What had she just witnessed?

"Here, now. Let us help you," the white woman said, kneeling beside her. A silver cross dangled from a chain around her neck. She dug into a pack slung over her shoulder. "What's your name?"

"T-tommie."

The woman cocked her head. "Interesting name for a girl."

"Thomasina. Thomasina Caldwell."

"I'm Matilda, and that's Julia." She uncorked a glass bottle. "You have wounds on your neck that, if we don't treat them, will cause a great infection and you will die."

Tommie was startled by the bluntness of her words, but appreciated it as well. Who were these women? They had saved her, but to what end?

"Are you witches too?" That was the only explanation her brain could come up with for what Eliza was—had been. A witch. A monstrous witch like in the stories her Gran had told them.

"That wasn't a witch, Thomasina. That was something entirely different and evil." Matilda smiled kindly at her as Julia went through the other rooms. "We aren't witches. We're hunters. We find evil and eradicate it."

"But you used something to fight her—it." Tommie frowned. "Something like what she used on me."

Like what I used . . . somehow.

Matilda nodded. "Yes, but we will have to explain that later. Right now, I need to put this on your wounds. It will sting fiercely, and probably leave scars, but you will die without it."

Tommie moved the collar of her dress aside. It was damp and sticky with blood. Her blood. Her stomach roiled.

Matilda dribbled the contents of the bottle across her neck. Tommie hissed at the burn of it, but Matilda let her squeeze her hand as she murmured soothing words.

"No one else," Julia said, returning to them. "Did you come alone?" she asked Tommie.

"I was looking for my brother, James. She said he was out with Mr. Palmer, looking for a lost goat. But Barney and the cart weren't here, and I never saw James on the road and . . . and . . ."

A sob caught in her throat.

Matilda and Julia exchanged looks. Tommie could read their expressions as if they had shouted to each other. James was gone. Mr. Palmer as well. Dead. Killed by the thing that had called herself Eliza Palmer, just as she'd boasted.

"No," she said, shaking her head.

"I'm sorry, Tommie," Matilda said, squeezing her hand gently. "Let's get out of here."

They helped her to her feet. She went along with them because she had no other means to get herself moving. The grief and pain of losing James would come later, as it had with Mam and Da. For now, she walked with these women, numb, out into the fading day. It was still unnaturally silent in Speary Wood.

"You held that demon off well enough," Julia said.

Tommie nodded. Demon. That made more sense. As unreal and unbelievable as it was, it made sense. And she had used means similar to those of Matilda and Julia. Something that came from inside her, unknown until she'd needed it. Sadly, it had come too late to help James.

"I think you're like us, Thomasina," Matilda said in what Tommie now knew was her gentle, soothing way. "Would you like to learn more about what you can do?"

Tommie stopped on the bridge. Gert waited for her, ears

perked as if waiting for her answer. She looked at Matilda and Julia in turn. With James gone, she had no one to go back to. "Yes. Yes, I would."

PERHAPS YOU MISSED MY SIGNS

---

by Anna Burke

THE WITCH NEVER WENT OUT of her way to eat children. Truthfully, she didn't even like them. They were too stringy, and the meat reminded her of the wild boar she fed in the winters from her cupped hands. One didn't eat one's friends. But "needs must," as her mother had been fond of saying, back in the mists of her youth.

You would think, she reflected now, that isolating one's self in the heart of a vast, tangled wood was a decent strategy for avoiding not only children, but also adults, adolescents, infants, the elderly, and all stages of human growth in between. And yet, an absurd number of them still wandered into her clearing.

Where had she gone wrong? She tapped her chin, eyeing her cottage. Vines framed the doorway, sharp with thorns. Candles flickered in the windows, casting a ghostly glow over the twilit garden. Night-blooming flowers tilted their faces toward the first of the stars. Sure, the smell of baking wafted from the chimney, but she had to eat, didn't she? It wasn't a crime to bake bread, and she dearly loved the way wild cherries flavored the crust when soaked in honey.

Did she need more signage? Were the skulls and bones not warning enough? Had the grubby little monsters gone blind as well as stupid? Or perhaps she needed to bewitch the trees to clack their branches even more ominously whenever humans passed her borders. Maybe she could convince a murder of crows to live up to their name, or at least flock in thicker circles. Surely there was *some* way she could deter trespassers. A moat? That would disturb too many roots, however, and then she'd have to reroute a river, find some nasty fanged fish to populate it, and spend hours of her days worried about algal blooms. No. A moat was not the solution.

A dragon? But dragons attracted knights, and knights had an unpleasant habit of thinking any women they encountered belonged to them, regardless of the opinions of the women in question. Plus, she hated disposing of their armor. There was only so much cutlery one witch could use in one immortal lifetime, and she'd knives and spoons aplenty.

Perhaps a basilisk. But again, knights.

That was the problem with humans. The more dangerous you made yourself, the more they seemed drawn to you, which said something about the survival instincts of the species. It was almost like they *wanted* to be eaten.

Her familiar sniffed the air. He was a small bear; he barely came over her head when he stood on his hind legs, and age had grizzled his black muzzle, but his claws remained as sharp as ever—ideal for breaking open wild beehives and ribcages alike.

"There, there," she said to him. "There's still time for them to turn back."

Down the winding forest path, past the stakes with their skulls and the "Trespassers Beware" signs written in every language she could think of, complete with pictorials for the illiterate, she heard the unmistakable sound of a child's laughter.

The real trouble, she decided as she scratched her familiar behind a scarred ear, was that humans didn't feed their young enough. Hungry woodcutters' spawn were drawn by the smells wafting from her oven, their eyes seeing only the promise of a meal at the end of the road and not the macabre displays. Even the life-size diorama she'd built, featuring an adult skeleton dressed in her old clothes, a cauldron whose bottom had rusted out once and for all despite her best efforts, and the three child-size skeletons arranged in various positions (one in the cauldron, one in a stone oven, and the other with its hands raised as if in fright) didn't catch their attention. *Idiots.*

She'd tried feeding the spawn a few centuries back, when she was younger and Arabella, her wife, still lived. Arabella had a soft spot for babies of all species. They'd even raised a few humans together, caring for them until they died from old age. All but the last. Arabella had begged the witch to let the girl return to her parents after the child had wept for a solid year. Against her better judgment, for humans were prejudiced creatures with a penchant for pitchforks and torches where witches were concerned, she had given in. She'd never been able to deny Arabella anything. And for Arabella's kindness?

Well. The tree in the center of her garden swayed in the soft evening breeze. It was all she had left of her, now. Even witches could be killed by a sufficiently determined mob.

The sound of childish voices grew louder. Two of them—a brother and a sister, if she cared to guess, which she did not. The bear grumbled. She let out a resigned sigh.

"Good thing I sharpened the knives yesterday."

Disemboweling was messy work, but she wasn't about to waste good meat, even if they were too gamy for her taste. Perhaps they'd be more palatable baked into a pie?

"Look," the boy said. "A cottage!"

"Do you smell that?" said the girl. "It smells like heaven."

The witch sighed again.

"For you, my dears, it will be."

GHOST WRITER

by Ann McMan

> "At present, I myself do not know of any local witches or warlocks, but there are several people who seem to have an uncanny power over food."
>
> –M.F.K. Fisher

MY NAME IS KIP, and I'm a ghost writer.

If that sounds to you like an introduction at a 12-Step meeting, you're not far from wrong. For me, it's a phrase that's always felt more like an apology than a description. Probably because the truth it evokes is a reminder of how the outcome of my poor life choices stained the family reputation like a broken sauce. That's because I didn't follow in my parents' footsteps– or *their* parents' footsteps. You see, I am descended from a long line of chefs—just like a secret recipe that's handed down for generations. The Kiplings have always been obsessed with food. And they're not simply obsessed like a teenager obsessed with scrolling on her iPhone, or a Malinois obsessed with finding the Ziploc bag of cocaine hidden inside a trash heap. Nope. In *my* family, food was like a fine marinade that enveloped you as soon as you escaped the amniotic fluid of the womb.

This is not to say I didn't try to toe the company line. I really did. But when it came to cooking, I just didn't have that umami gene—or any of the other essential taste receptors in the pantheon that all great chefs are supposed to be imbued with. I couldn't distinguish a nucleotide from a Necco wafer. So, after years of having the vending machine of life tell me to make another selection, I did. I became a photographer. Then a food stylist. Then a food writer.

One could argue that this fallen apple didn't roll too far away from the family tree. But being a freelance journalist wasn't rarified enough for my parents—not even when I started getting high-dollar gigs from top tier magazines like *Saveur* and *Garden & Gun*. They remained unimpressed.

Those who can, do. Those who can't, write about it and get paid by the inch.

I didn't bother to tell them that no one had been paid by the inch since Charles Dickens was sealing the fate of Little Nell. It was a nuance that would've carried about as much weight as a flake of Maldon Salt.

So, when my agent notified me that I'd been requested to work on the widely anticipated new cookbook by celebrated author Marguerite Steele, I jumped at the chance.

I mean . . . come on. *Marguerite Steele?* She was an epicurean legend—not to mention a total enigma. As far as I knew, next to no one had ever even met her. The woman staunchly refused to do live interviews or in-person appearances. She was renowned as a recluse who lived in some Podunk town off the beaten path in northern Vermont. Which, to be fair, didn't signify much when it came to talking about places in Vermont. Most of the locations in the state I'd ever visited had the town name painted on both sides of the sign.

But she had requested me. *By name*. That had to signify . . . *something*. Right? I mean . . . my parents would have to be impressed by this one.

Or so I thought.

It turned out that Marguerite Steele . . . wait for it . . . lived on a fricking *island* in the middle of Lake Champlain. *An island*. As in, only accessible by boat.

Okay. That gave rise to all manner of minor key vibrations. But as the boat slowed and drifted closer to her modest dock, I did my best to ignore them. It wasn't the weirdest thing in the world to have to travel by boat to the secluded island retreat of the world's most notoriously mercurial foodie . . . was it?

Was it?

Henri, the charter captain I'd hired to ferry me across the lake to Steele's Savage Island retreat, hopped out of the pontoon and tied off.

"*Nous voilà*," he said in French. "Savage Island. Home of the famous and feared Meg Steele."

"*Merci*." I grabbed hold of my backpack and stepped over onto the dock. The mainland looked different from this vantage point. Smaller. More like another . . . island—which it was. Just larger.

What the fuck with this place?

Vermont was supposed to be the Green Mountain State—not some damn French-speaking archipelago.

"You'll be back to pick me up at four?" I asked Henri.

"*Oui*." He smiled rakishly. "*A moins qu'elle ne te fasse revenir à la nage.*"

I looked at him with confusion.

"Unless Meg makes you *swim*." He winked at me and got back into the boat. "*Bonne chance!*"

Henri was wishing me good luck?

"*A plus tard.*" He gave me a small salute and shoved off.

I waved back at him before glancing up the winding path toward a modest-looking cottage covered with weathered gray shakes.

How bad could she be?

I watched while Henri pushed his pontoon away from the dock and began the short trip back to the marina at Keeler Bay. Then I hitched my bag up higher on my shoulder and began making my way up the rutted path toward the world's most hermitic chef.

"Probably one of the most private things in the world is an egg until it is broken."

–M.F.K. Fisher

Crumple. Whoosh. Bump.

I was sitting with Camille in the old solarium, which had been converted to a group ward about four months earlier, when the number of patients had grown beyond the limited capacity of the small hospital. Many families chose, instead, to send their loved ones to a larger care facility in Boston, but Camille's relatives did not possess the resources for that, and I would not leave her.

Crumple. Whoosh. Bump.

Late afternoon light was streaming in from the narrow windows that ringed the high ceiling. It broke the vacuous interior into dramatic shards that made the ward look striped—like someone had painted wide swaths of the cold space with burnt umber. I was reading to Camille, as had become our custom after my own therapy sessions were completed and I had a respite before returning to my own room for the evening.

Crumple. Whoosh. Bump.

For the better part of a week, I'd been sharing sections of introductory prose and recipes from the new M.F.K. Fisher cookbook I'd just received from my dear friend Laurent, who had procured it for me at Brentano's in Greenwich Village.

"It seems to me that our three basic needs, for food and security and love, are so mixed and mingled and entwined that we cannot straightly think of one without the other."

Crumple. Whoosh. Bump.

"So it happens that when I write of hunger, I am really writing about love and the hunger for it . . . and then the warmth and richness and fine reality of hunger satisfied . . . and it is all one."

Crumple. Whoosh. Bump.

"What was that Meg?"

Camille's voice seemed smaller than it had earlier. It, like the rest of her, was beginning to fade. To disappear. I had to strain to hear her over the noise of the machine.

I held up the book. "It's M.F.K. Fisher. *The Gastronomical Me.*"

Crumple. Whoosh. Bump.

"I like it. It's not just about food, is it?"

I had to think for a moment about how to reply to her. In fact, I had picked today's passage for precisely that reason. The truth was I wanted the author's words to tell Camille the things I was too timid to say for myself, for fear she would reject me.

"No," I agreed. "It's about everything."

Crumple. Whoosh. Bump.

"Everything." Her voice was soft, like a whisper.

I bent closer so I could see her narrow face, bathed in amber light, reflected in the mirror fixed just above her head.

"Camille?" She did not reply. "Camille? *Dors-tu?*"

She was silent. There was no sound except the rhythmic *crumple, whoosh, bump* of the machine that was breathing for her.

> "Having bowed to the inevitability of the dictum that we must eat to live, we should ignore it and live to eat."
>
> –M.F.K. Fisher

"You must be Alice."

It wasn't a question. And the woman standing before me like the presiding judge at a court-martial didn't look like she'd ever admit to being wrong if I weren't, in fact, Alice.

"Actually," I dared to suggest, "my name is Kip." I took a tighter grip on the strap of my backpack. It was heavy, and it didn't seem like I'd be putting it down anytime soon.

"Kip?" She didn't seem convinced. And her French accent made the word sound alien—like she was saying "keep." In fact, her expression was downright . . . dubious. "As in, *kipper?*"

"No. As in *Kipling*. It's a nickname." I smiled. "For Alice."

"Étrange. How very singular."

I didn't know if the "singular" aspect was the name itself, or the concept of nicknames in general.

"It was a childhood name that stuck." I shrugged in mute apology for my family's complete lack of obeisance to decorum by allowing me to adopt an apparently ridiculous nickname.

She didn't comment on my lame explanation.

"Allez, suivez-moi. Follow me." She pointed up the path. "To the house."

She turned on her low heels and headed back up the path toward the house. I looked her over as she strode on ahead of me.

Who the fuck besides Mrs. Howell wore heels on a damn island?

She had a curious kind of gait, too—not very fluid, but certainly determined. It wasn't a limp exactly. But more like she had to consider how she undertook each stride. I figured it was probably the result of having to learn how to walk around on the uneven terrain of this island. Apart from that, she looked pretty . . . well . . . kind of *hot*, actually. Quirky—but stylish. Dressed in a sort of retro-looking ensemble that hinted at 1950s chic. She wasn't at all what I expected, based on the apocryphal rumors about her eccentricity. I had no idea how old she was. Thirty-five? Forty? Even forty-five? It was impossible to tell. She had blondish hair streaked with gray. And she was a small woman, which surprised me for someone with her fierce reputation. She couldn't have been much over five feet tall. Well-built and compact-looking, too, with curves in all the right places.

It almost made me want to overlook her irascibility.

She abruptly turned her head and glared at me, as if she'd been able to divine the direction of my thoughts.

Almost . . .

When we entered the kitchen of her small cottage, Marguerite waved me toward a seat at her antique farmhouse table. It was a beast of a creation with oversized trestle legs and a scrubbed top made of French oak. It must've weighed more than a thousand pounds. I wondered what the hell kind of boat had ferried that thing out to her island.

"*Asseyez-vous.*" When I didn't budge, she appeared annoyed at having to translate. "Sit down . . . please."

The tacked-on "please" felt like a reluctant postscript. I dropped my bag to the floor and pulled out a chair. The kitchen was impressively equipped. She had an enormous Bertazzoni six-burner range with two ovens—tastefully dazzling in matte black.

I supposed she thought the color of the high-powered behemoth made the kitchen look . . . *slimmer.*

"Nice place."

She didn't seem impressed by my observation. "Thank you."

"I gather this is where we'll be working."

"*Évidemment.*"

Even I knew what that meant.

"How shall we begin?"

She crossed the room and retrieved a thick sheaf of papers

from a sideboard before joining me at the table.

"I thought we should review these recipes together to see if you have any questions before attempting to recreate them and adding your own edits and notes to the narrative." She pushed the tower of paper toward me.

Recreate them? I sifted through the pages. There had to be at least a hundred pages of recipes.

"You must be joking. We're making *all* of these?"

"No. We aren't." She appeared unfazed. "*You* are."

"Me?" I was flabbergasted. "That's crazy. I cannot possibly cook this many dishes. I can barely boil water."

"Did you not read your contract, Alice?"

"I don't recall any language about having to recreate *this* many recipes." I stopped flipping through the pages of single-spaced type and looked at her. "And it's Kip. Not Alice."

"I discussed all these particulars in detail with your agent, Alice. I regret she did not share them with you."

This was getting me no place. "How do you say, 'that sucks' in French?"

She looked perplexed by my question. "*C'est chiant.*"

"Yeah . . ." I pointed at her. "What you just said."

If I didn't know better, I'd swear she nearly smiled. Sadly, I did know better. But I was curious about something else.

"Who on earth did this work for you on your other cookbooks?"

She didn't seem to find my curiosity impertinent—which I half expected.

"A colleague of mine, Laurent Bouchard."

"If I might ask, why is he not working with you on this one?"

She took a moment before answering. "Laurent passed away last April."

"Oh." I felt like a schmuck. "I'm sorry. That must've been difficult for you."

"*C'est le moins qu'on puisse dire*. . . it was. We collaborated on many books. And he was . . . *un ami cher.* A dear friend."

"I lost a good friend recently, too—the features editor at *Bon*

Appétit, who took a chance on me and gave me my start. I owed everything to him. So, I know how hard it is to lose someone who matters. I'm very sorry for your loss."

"*Merci* . . . Kip."

Shit . . . *a breakthrough.*

Marguerite inched her chair a bit closer to mine. She smelled good. Like jasmine and—something else. Oranges? It was a faint but pleasing scent. Not cloying. Subtle. Unobtrusive. It was obvious she knew how to wear it.

"How about we look through these recipes together?" she suggested. "To see if you have any questions or concerns."

I smiled at her. "Good idea. With luck, we should manage to get through them all before the lake freezes over."

She looked perplexed. "It's . . . *June?*"

"Yeah." I pushed the pages over, so the stack sat between us. "I know."

She looked away from me and slowly shook her head.

And this time—I was sure she had to work to hide her smile.

> "An oyster leads a dreadful but exciting life.
> Indeed, his chance to live at all is slim.
> Life is hard, we say. An oyster's life is worse."
>
> –M.F.K. Fisher

The three Fates of Greek mythology had been reborn as the three variants of the polio virus.

Brunhilde. Lanchi. Leon.

The Spinner, the Allotter, and the Inflexible were now presiding over the inescapable destinies of more than 50,000 of us. These three fates of the epidemic had become the mad determiners of who would succumb and who would survive this plague.

After I was diagnosed, it was Laurent who retrieved me from my island retreat and drove me south to enter the small treatment facility at Mary Fletcher Hospital in Burlington. I'd been told that my escalating symptoms—headache, fatigue, stomach upset, and muscle tenderness in my right calf—indicated that I was in the pre-paralytic stage, so time was of the essence. My doctor predicted I might respond well to the treatment regimen developed by the Australian bush nurse, Sister Kenny. And I had the advantage of being able to afford enrollment in some of the clinical trials that were being tested on patients like me, who were afflicted by Lanchi, the Allotter.

Sadly, that was not true for everyone.

Laurent picked me up at the marina in Keeler Bay. The drive south to Mary Fletcher would take us less than an hour.

"You should be in Boston," Laurent scolded me. "They have better doctors. More treatment innovations—immunotherapies that are yielding good results for non-bulbar patients."

I resisted his entreaties.

"Camille is here," I explained.

Laurent slapped his hand on the steering wheel of his ancient Renault Quintette. "*Pourquoi es-tu si obstinée?*"

"I am not being stubborn. I will not leave her." I touched his hand to steady it. *"Tu le sais bien."*

He looked at me with sadness. *"Oui."*

We drove slowly along old US 2, a route that wound its way in and out through the small towns that dotted the lakefront. It was mid-October. Dried red and yellow leaves swirled and skittered around us in a bold and frenzied pastiche of color—nature's last gasp of brilliance before the onset of what promised to be a long and brutal winter.

"Does she know?"

Laurent's question startled me. The directness of it caught me off guard.

"Know what?" I didn't need to ask who he was asking about.

"Que tu l'aimes."

That I love her . . . I saw no reason to lie to him.

"Non."

As Laurent's car ate up the miles between one shopworn Vermont town and the next, I was lost in a jumbled disarray of thoughts: certain of one thing, but completely at sea about everything else. I could not imagine or begin to enumerate all the ways my life would surely change—or even if I would emerge from the experience able to recognize myself.

Or might I, like Camille, have to face the prospect that there might be no life remaining for me beyond my internment at Mary Fletcher?

"Nous sommes arrivés."

Laurent's voice startled me.

A castellated mansion loomed before us like a dark vision.

My descent into hell was at hand.

> "Sharing food with another human being is an intimate act that should not be indulged in lightly."
>
> –M.F.K. Fisher

"*This is unacceptable!* You have now burned the shallots, thrice."

"Thrice?" I quoted.

"Oui."

Her ridiculous intensity and use of the antiquated word struck me as funny—even though nothing about the murderous look she was giving me was remotely humorous. I started to laugh. And the more bewildered my laughing made her, the less I could control it. It was exactly like being at the opera and realizing you were about to cough—and nothing you could do would prevent it or diminish its intensity. Especially the dirty looks you were getting from the octogenarians in the seats beside you.

Marguerite was furiously cleaning the sauté pan . . . for the third time.

"I fail to see the humor in a wealth of burned shallots."

"You don't?"

"*Non.*"

"Strange. I find burned shallots to be inordinately funny."

She all but glowered at me. "I do wish you could take this enterprise more seriously."

"What part of this enterprise do you think I have *not* taken seriously? I've been wrestling with these infernal goat cheese creations of yours for five days now. And I've filled at least a ream of paper with pithy and erudite notes about the recipes—only a *third* of which you've completely rewritten."

"You find this *frustrant?*"

I cupped an ear.

"Annoying," she translated.

"No. I wouldn't say annoying, exactly. But it is certainly making me peckish."

"Peckish?" She asked. "Why peckish?"

"I dunno. Must be the fourth stomach . . . ."

She gave me a withering look. It was one of her good ones. I'd seen enough of them over the last week to be able to discriminate.

"As I have already explained to you . . . *thrice* . . . my cookbooks are thematic." Marguerite warmed to her line of attack. "*Le fromage de chèvre* is an internationally popular ingredient because of its suitability for people with low tolerance for cow's milk. And its creamy texture and fruity notes make it a superb addition to many recipes. Not to mention, it's high in protein and low in fat for the dietary conscious."

"Undoubtedly."

"You find that amusing?"

"I hadn't really thought about it until right now. But yes. I'd definitely be tempted to call one hundred forty-seven recipes featuring goat cheese as a primary ingredient *amusing.*"

Marguerite faced me with her hands on her hips. "If you

find this assignment so onerous, perhaps you should ask your agent to gain your release from our contract."

"I don't have to do that. If you don't want me to continue working with you, you can just fire me." I smiled at her. "It won't be the first time."

"*Moi?* I never said anything about wanting to fire you."

"Not even after I burned the shallots . . . thrice?"

Marguerite shook her head and crossed the kitchen to open the outside door. Once again, I noticed her oddly circular gait.

"Where are you going?" I called after her.

She didn't look back at me. "To get more shallots."

While she was out of the room, I took advantage of her absence to slip a bogus recipe into the working manuscript pages of her cookbook. I knew that when our time together had finished and she sat down to conduct her final review of the work we'd done together, she'd find it. I hoped when she did, it would make her smile. I didn't know if she'd remember me with fondness, as I knew I would remember her—but I hoped she might at least be able to recall me with something approaching amusement.

Three hours—and only one additional incinerated shallot—later, I had successfully completed the current section on savory brunch recipes featuring chèvre and eggs—or *œufs*, as she called them. I must've been developing a tolerance for the pungent cheese because several of the dishes tasted almost . . . decent.

"Try this." I held a bite of the Goat Cheese Mousse Crostini out to Marguerite. But she demurred, as always. I continued to find it extremely odd that she steadfastly refrained from tasting anything I cooked. It seemed counterintuitive to me. How was she to know if I'd managed to prepare the dishes accurately if she never tried them? I asked her about it . . . again.

"I need to be able to rely upon the sensibilities of the home chef to determine if the recipes are correctly prepared," she explained. "That is a nuance that exists separate from my own preconceived ideas about how things should taste."

I lowered the fork. "You do realize that nothing about this

approach even remotely makes sense. Right?"

"I fail to see why this bothers you so much. Laurent was never so . . . insistent."

"Maybe that's because I'm less refined?"

She shrugged but made no reply. It wasn't the first time we'd had the same conversation.

I ate the bite of crostini. To my unrefined palate—and to the honor of the shallots that had bravely given their lives to get us to this happy place—the dish tasted pretty damn good.

"Okay then," I told her. "I think we're there on this one."

"Bien. C'est tout ce que je veux savoir." Before I could ask, she translated. "Good. That's what I want to know."

Once it was clear we'd reached détente on the success of my repeated efforts, it was time to photograph the finished dish. In this area, at least, Marguerite assisted me to ensure the plating matched her expectations. I took several test photos using my handheld exposure meter to be sure the lighting level was appropriate. Marguerite preferred to have the dishes photographed *in situ,* versus moving them to an area where I could better command the variables. So, we'd constructed a makeshift staging area atop her massive French oak table.

Once everything, including relevant peripherals like flatware, a glass of the correct wine, and decorative smatterings of fresh herbs and flowers were artfully displayed, Marguerite would retreat from the scene, and I would begin to frame and capture the images.

Although I owned a high-quality digital camera, I preferred to use film for natural light environments like Marguerite's kitchen. Film was ideally suited to situations where there was a greater risk of overexposure. The only downside was having to wait to process the images, since I didn't have access to a darkroom in these infernal islands. That meant I had to arrange time to travel to Burlington to use a photo lab located in the design school at UVM. I arranged with Marguerite in advance to take a full day next week to process the film I'd already shot and make contact prints of the images for her review. With luck, there wouldn't be many we'd need to revisit. I did not relish the idea of having to remake any of the goat cheese-laden dishes.

After I'd finished taking the photos, we began to clear away the mess I'd created cooking the day's recipes. We'd fallen into a natural rhythm doing this. I scraped plates and wiped out pans and stacked them tidily on the counter beside her sink. She then would painstakingly wash and rinse each one of them and leave them for me to dry and return to their rightful resting places on the open shelves in her kitchen. I also returned all the unused butter, eggs, cream, and ubiquitous logs of goat cheese to her bright blue Smeg refrigerator. The thing was packed to the gills with all the cold ingredients we used to prepare the recipes. I figured she must keep a second fridge to accommodate her personal food items in some other location.

As was her custom, Marguerite made sure to wrap up the best examples of the food I'd cooked that day.

"You can take this with you," she had directed the first time she did this. "And eat it later—or share it with Henri."

I had tried to argue with her on that first occasion. But it proved pointless, just like all disagreements with Marguerite.

"Don't you want to keep some of this to eat yourself?"

"Pourquoi?" she'd ask. "Why?"

"Because it's good and you might enjoy it."

"I don't need to keep it. I already know what it tastes like."

Yeah. Okay. Whatever, lady . . .

I did share the first few days' worth of dishes with Henri. And he was most appreciative.

"Laurent was never so generous," he pointed out. "For more than thirty years, I ferried him over here, day after day, while the two of them hammered out Meg's best books. And not once did he ever offer me so much as a taste of what they'd concocted inside those cottage walls. *"C'était dommage."*

As the days went by, however, I found myself sharing less and less of the leftover food with Henri—not because I didn't like him. I did. He was an affable fellow and a first-class boat captain. I enjoyed our daily lake voyages together. But I found myself, reluctantly, beginning to enjoy eating the quirky food and becoming less inclined to share it, and that was a real shock since I'd never been a fan of goat cheese. I'd always found its taste to be too . . . *goaty*.

It was irksome to have to admit that the redoubtable Marguerite Steele was really onto something with these eclectic approaches to her bestselling cookbooks.

But I was determined never to tell *her* that . . .

I collected my little parcel of goat cheese creations and prepared to take my leave for the day. A thought occurred to me.

"Why does Henri call you Meg?"

"Excuse-moi?"

"Henri. He calls you Meg, not Marguerite. I was just curious about that."

"It's a nickname," she explained, before giving me a half smile. "Like Kip."

"Oh. Good to know." I walked toward the door. "Goodnight, Meg."

I didn't hear her reply until I was halfway out the door.

"*Bonsoir*, Kip."

> "I cannot count the good people I know who,
> to my mind, would be even better if they bent
> their spirits to the study of their own hungers."
>
> –M.F.K. Fisher

"Sadly, that's how this virus works: *quickly*. In the space of a day or two, you can go from having a headache to being unable to walk." In my initial meeting with him, Dr. Edison made it clear that I should not tarry reporting to Mary Fletcher—although his preference was that I travel to Boston for treatment. "We won't know the type or likely extent of your infection until we get the results of your throat culture."

"But you suspect it is not bulbar?" I'd been thinking about Camille's diagnosis.

"I do. Your clinical presentations are not yet indicative of that. For one thing, your symptoms, while concerning, are less progressive."

I explained to him that Laurent was delivering me to the Burlington hospital on Friday. I did not share with him that my refusal to travel to Boston was because my childhood friend, Camille Overleaux, was being treated at Mary Fletcher. That wouldn't have been a compelling enough reason for him. In fact, he probably would've scoffed at it and told me not to be ridiculous.

Dr. Edison was a good friend of my father's, and that familiarity led him to feel free to express strong opinions without much attention to decorum or editorial restraint.

Besides, I didn't think intimate details about my relationship with Camille—and all it was or wasn't—was any of his, or anyone else's, business.

The truth was, the Steele and Overleaux families had known each other for generations. My mother, Isabelle Overleaux, was a distant cousin of Camille's father, Georges. My father met her when he was working in Montreal for the Grand Trunk Railway, which later was absorbed when threats of wartime and domestic emergencies led to the nationalization of Canada's rail system. After marrying, my parents lived in Montreal until I was ten. Then my father took a position with the New York Central Railroad, and we moved to Albany. But our two families remained very close, and the Steeles and Overleaux vacationed together every summer in the Champlain Islands of Vermont.

That was how Camille and I became fast friends. And how I grew to love her.

Camille had always loved music, and had grown up to become a fine clarinetist, performing with several esteemed chamber ensembles in Quebec. Her goal had been to study orchestral music, and she enrolled at McGill after finishing secondary school. My interests had always centered around food. The simple fact was that I wanted to be a chef—even though it was not a role traditionally open to women. But I persisted and eventually wore my parents down. After years of apprenticeships at restaurants in New York and Boston, I finally had amassed enough experience to gain admission to Le Cordon Bleu in Paris. My mother had a dear friend living there, and she consented to house me during my ten-month tenure at the esteemed academy.

During our final summer in the islands, Camille and I spent every waking hour together, dreaming about our futures and the fantastic lives we would lead after completing our professional courses of study. After breakfast, we would carry our towels, our books, and our tin boxes containing Pippin apples, my mother's homemade crackers, and fresh sharp cheddar cheese curds from the Wimble dairy farm down to the sandy beach on the south end of the island. There we would stay, swimming, reading, and sunning the entire day until we were called back to help lay the table for dinner.

It was on a hot July day that I became dramatically aware of how my feelings for Camille had changed. One afternoon, while we were swimming, Camille got a cramp in her calf and began to panic and flail in the deep water near the jagged cliffs. The lake was choppy that day because it had rained overnight, and the currents were stronger and more insistent than normal. We shouldn't have been swimming at all, but the heat of the sun had led us to suspend better judgment and seek relief in the cooler waters of the south end. When I heard her cry out in pain and saw her distress, I swam as fast as the waves would allow to reach her. I was terrified watching her struggle to remain afloat. Panicked thoughts pounded inside my head. *Don't let her drown. Don't let her drown. Blessed Virgin, please let me reach her. Don't let her drown. I love her. I love her.*

When I reached her, she grabbed onto me with such a vise-like grip that I had to fight to keep us both afloat. I feared that her desperation would take both of us under. In that split second,

I nearly wished she would—for I understood that the depth of the passion I felt for her would never be requited. I knew, in the way your self-understanding can suddenly reveal itself before you like an asteroid streaking across the night sky, that I was in love with her. That I had been for years. And in those first moments of panic and struggle, I thought it would be better for me to die with her, than to live and face a lifetime without her.

Camille didn't die that day. I was able to calm her enough to slowly lead her to the shore. We sat together on the sand for what felt like hours—not speaking, until our breathing returned to normal and the cramping in her leg subsided. Camille then thanked me over and over for saving her. I brushed off her expressions of gratitude, afraid she might look at me too closely. Terrified she might hear the screaming laments of my heart. Anxious to do anything but mortify myself by allowing her to see my weakness—or risk having her reject me because of how I feared she might view my unnatural affection for her.

We never talked about the events of that day again. I told Camille it was my wish, and after much argument, she finally capitulated and agreed to respect my wishes, even though she did not understand them. It was unspoken, but we both understood that we were sharing something magical during our final weeks together on Savage Island. We talked endlessly about our hopes for the future. Our plans for our lives after college and culinary school. About where we wanted to live. What adventures we'd have. What intrigues. What romantic entanglements. And we vowed *always* to remain in each other's lives—and promised to reunite every summer for another enchanted stay at our beloved paradise in the Champlain Islands.

Little did I know then how our darkly fabled story was destined to unfold.

"It is all a question of weeding out what you yourself like best to do, so that you can live most agreeably in a world full of an increasing number of disagreeable surprises."

–M.F.K. Fisher

Henri and I were seated in a dark, corner booth at the local public house, enjoying our pints of Hill's Sail Pale Ale, one of the pub's signature microbrews. It had been my idea to stop off there after Henri had fetched me from Savage Island. I enjoyed his company. He was a salty old fellow who'd been ferrying people around these islands longer than I'd been alive. I loved listening to the snippets of island lore—and gossip—he was always willing to share. Stories and rumors he'd gleaned from disgruntled local business owners, seasonal residents, and an endless parade of tourists.

I suppose the writer in me was enough of a voyeur to revel in Henri's easy camaraderie and willingness to dish on the storied lives of his fellow islanders. And, to be fair, I was more than a little bit curious about the background of one of the area's most peculiar residents.

After our second round—it was a Vermont Session IPA this time—I decided to ask him outright to come clean about Meg. It was a Friday night—the end of what had been an especially taxing week. Meg had been characteristically demanding, pushing me to plow my way through the last twelve recipes in her section on appetizers and *amuse-bouches*.

Who ever knew that banging out two dozen perfect, bite-sized portions of anything could be so fricking onerous?

By the time we'd finished up, I was ready to throw both Meg *and* the platter of fucking goat-infused *amuse-bouches* into the sanctified waters of Lake Champlain. And I was more determined than ever to get Henri to dish about the obstreperous chef.

I pushed our basket of pretzel bites and hot beer cheese closer to him.

"I thought you told me you knew Laurent, Meg's previous collaborator," I reminded him. "What was he like?"

"Très arrogant." Henri didn't mince words. "Pompous."

"You didn't like him?"

"*Non.* He treated me like *un sous-fifre*—a servant. And he never tipped." He popped a pretzel bite into his mouth. *"Radin."*

I was glad I'd already handed our server my credit card.

"You said you took him to the island many times—over many years."

"Oui." He nodded. "At least thirty years."

Thirty years? To work with Meg? But that would be impossible. Meg couldn't be more than forty. Fifty at most, although that seemed like a stretch. For Laurent to have been working with her on her cookbooks for thirty years, she'd have to be . . .

I racked my brain to recall when Meg's first cookbook was published. *Was it in the mid-1980s? Even earlier?* I wasn't sure.

But nothing about this math was adding up.

I pressed Henri. "Are you sure about taking Laurent to the island to work with Meg?"

"Oui. Who else?"

"Did you ever see her when you dropped him off?"

He thought about it. "Only from a distance. She never came down to the dock."

I knew he was right about that. Meg rarely ventured more than a few yards from her house. I'd tried to interest her before in going for a walk on the island, just to break up the monotony of nonstop cooking. But she had always refused. I'd just assumed it had something to do with her desire to finish our work as quickly as possible so she could be rid of me.

But maybe that wasn't it . . .

My head was still reeling. How the hell old *was* Marguerite Steele?

"Does Meg ever leave the island?" Until that moment, it had never occurred to me that I'd never noticed any kind of boat at her place—not tied to her dock, or moored anyplace else within sight.

Henri shook his head. "Not that I'm aware of. I deliver

her groceries and other supplies about twice a month. I have strict orders to leave things in a small shed at the base of her walkway. She leaves payment for me in an envelope. *En espèces.*" He smiled. "Cash."

"Does she tip?" I teased.

"*Oui.* Madame Meg is most generous."

"Any other visitors or family ever show up out there?"

"Are you here to investigate her?" Henri narrowed his eyes as he regarded me. "Were you hired by someone? *Le gouvernement?*"

"No. Of course not."

"*Je suis confus.* Why all the questions then?"

I was surprised by his defensive tone. "Oh, come on, Henri. Are you saying it's *never* occurred to you to wonder how this woman, who doesn't look a day over forty-five, and who never leaves that island, could possibly have been writing and publishing cookbooks since around 1985 . . . more than thirty-eight years ago?"

"*Non.*"

"No?" I didn't believe him for an instant. "Impossible."

"*Impossible?*" He leaned toward me. "We don't know anything about what is impossible."

"What the hell is that supposed to mean?"

"It means, my dear friend, that there are more things in heaven and earth than are dreamt of in your imagination."

"Yeah," I corrected him. "That's my *philosophy*—not my imagination. And I saw *Hamlet,* thank you very much. So, nice try. And Meg is no shrinking violet, under the spell of an evil puppet master—believe me."

"We don't know what Meg is."

I was intrigued by the bluntness of his statement. "Who is we?"

He gestured toward the big room full of people. "All of us. Everyone here."

"You're telling me that no one in this community has ever bothered to ask these questions about the strange inhabitant of Savage Island?"

"*Oui.*"

I shook my head in wonder. "How is that possible?"

"We live by different rules here. We make no judgments. She does no harm to anyone." He shrugged. "She pays her bills. Her life is her own—as are her secrets—and her mysteries. We respect that. And so should you." He drained his glass. "A final round before we bid each other *bonne nuit?*"

He signaled our waiter.

I didn't know what I'd been expecting to hear from Henri when I first started this line of inquiry—maybe just a bit of salacious gossip about his late-night work ferrying jilted lovers away after Meg had finished with them. But I never could've predicted where my questions would lead. My thoughts were whirling like a crazed dervish. *How had I managed to miss so many clues?* And who in the hell *was* this woman?

Even more to the point: *what* was she?

And why did it suddenly matter so much to me to find out?

And that question was destined to haunt me more than any of the others that were conspiring to keep me awake throughout the long night ahead.

> "... when two people are able to weave that kind of invisible thread of understanding and sympathy between each other, they should not risk tearing it. It is too rare, and it lasts too short a time at best ..."
>
> –M.F.K. Fisher

I had been at Mary Fletcher for more than two months. During that time, my daily therapies continued and my condition, if it did not dramatically improve, at least grew no worse. I was luckier than most. It became difficult to reconcile my good fortune with the ill fortunes of so many others. The wards were filled with patients—most of them children. It was a grueling reminder of the harsh and heedless way the virus moved through our communities like a brutal assassin, wildly striking out at the least among us and felling them with reckless abandon. Only occasionally did adults fall prey to its cruel ascendency. And, sadly, we enjoyed fewer positive outcomes.

Regrettably, my Camille became heir to a near-hopeless prognosis. Her time in the iron lung steadily increased until she was spending most hours of the day and night inside her noisy prison. She had become encased in a cruel exoskeleton that she'd never be able to shed. The reality of her plight did not escape me, although I tried valiantly to deny it—at least in my daily vigils with her. Whether or not she fully understood the dire circumstances and likely duration of her confinement was unclear. She never spoke of it. But Camille never spoke about anything that was difficult or unpleasant—not even when she was at McGill, and had to learn Bartók's *Miraculous Mandarin* for a solo recital before the faculty review committee. She did it, of course, in her characteristic, quiet way. And she played it superbly. I know, because I'd just returned from Paris and watched from a seat in the very back of the darkened hall. I never told Camille I was there. I hadn't wanted her to endure that added pressure.

I had never told Camille many things that I knew might unsettle her. I still didn't. And I knew I was running out of time to change that.

We sat together one late afternoon in the old solarium. Camille had had a difficult day. Her breathing, even with the assistance of the big machine, was stertorous and ragged. She seemed unfocused and vague. What should have been the simple act of drawing a single breath became a marathon that taxed and exhausted her. I wanted to leave her so she could rest, but she begged me to stay by her side.

"Not yet." I had to bend closer to hear her. Her eyes were glassy, yet they met mine with marked intensity. "Stay with me." A breath. "Longer."

So I stayed. She wanted me to talk. To tell her stories.

"What stories, *ma chère?* You have heard them all. Many times."

"About . . ." A ragged breath. "About you." Another painful breath. "About Paris."

"About Paris?" I was confused.

"Yes." A breath. "About Le . . ." Another gasp for air. "Le . . ."

"Le Cordon Bleu? You want me to tell you about culinary school?"

She didn't try to speak. But she smiled. The effort it took was so difficult for her, I wanted to cry. To scream. To drag myself through the wards on my twisted leg and smash anything I could get my hands on in a frenzy of anguish and protest. To rage against this madness. It wasn't fair. It wasn't right. *It made no sense.* And we were all powerless to stop it. All we could do was sit together in in our fear and isolation. A lost community of beleaguered Jobs, scratching at our boils and begging God to explain why he'd forsaken us.

"It was 1950. I had just arrived and was staying in a flat with Delphine Dumont, my mother's roommate from Laval. Delphine lived on the third floor of a building in the 7th Arrondissement, near the Eiffel Tower. It was while shopping for cooking supplies at E. Dehillerin in Les Halles that I first met Julia. She would've been impossible to miss in any setting—she towered over everyone. Of course, I had no idea who she was at that point, but I sensed that one day everyone would know her. I'd been deliberating for some time over which sauce whisk was best when a hand appeared in front of me holding a longish-handled model with a soft balloon head.

"This one," she said with her curious, almost garbled accent. "I've tried them all."

I looked up at her gratefully. She had a friendly set to her features, with welcoming brown eyes.

"Merci, Madame." I took the whisk from her. "I am starting culinary school tomorrow and feel quite out of my depth."

She smiled. "At Le Cordon Bleu?" When I nodded, she continued. "Don't let those snobby bastards scare you. Stand right up to them and let them know you have as much right to be there as they do. Refuse to be intimidated."

"Snobby . . . bastards." Camille repeated. "I love that."

My heart melted. *"Oui. Je sais."*

"Tell me . . ." She didn't continue.

I wondered for a moment if Camille was finally asking me to tell her the truth about my long-held feelings. But I knew it wasn't that. She wanted me to go on with my story.

"I later found out that Julia had just finished her six months of training at Le Cordon Bleu and was now taking private lessons with chef Max Bugnard. But I saw her from time to time, out with her beloved husband, Paul—and once, dining on platters of fat Brittany oysters at La Couronne with her friend Simone Beck. She always recognized me, even though we'd only spoken that one time. She'd smile and reflexively whip her hand around in tight, controlled arcs—as if to ask if my whisk was still performing as it should." I slowly shook my head and smiled at the recollection. "I never forgot her, and I never shall. And mostly because she never forgot *me*."

I looked down at Camille to share my sweet memory. Her eyes were closed. I thought she'd somehow managed to fall asleep. Then I noticed that something about the timbre of the machine had changed. No. *It wasn't the machine.* It was working as it always did, without fail, day and night. What had changed was Camille.

She was no longer breathing.

I began to panic—to rise up and cry out for help. But I didn't. I sank back against my chair and studied her features. They were . . . calm. At peace. The months of pain and hardship had evaporated from her face. She looked younger. More vital. Less like an invalid and more like . . . *Camille*. More like the young and confident prodigy who'd stood before packed audiences and played her clarinet with energy, ease, and perfect breath control. In that final moment of release, she became the consummate fulfillment of who she'd always been. She was complete and without blemish. She was free.

And she was gone from me forever.

"Je t'aimerai toujours," I whispered.

I continued to sit with her in lost and bewildered silence—alone and adrift with my yearning and an ensuing lifetime of lost hope.

> "For me there is too little of life to spend most of it forcing myself into detachment from it."
>
> –M.F.K. Fisher

After I finished working my way through Meg's recent edits to my recipe narratives, I spent the rest of Saturday in the dark, sealed up inside a photo lab at UVM. I cursed myself for waiting so long to process all the film I'd shot in the two weeks Meg and I had been cooking together. We'd done an ungodly amount of work. It was staggering actually. I'd creamed, whipped, crumbled, and folded so much damn goat cheese I was beginning to eye the infernal creatures differently whenever I caught sight of them bumbling around in the field that ran behind my small hotel.

That one's really nice looking, I'd think. *I like the way it won't take any shit off those other two. I wonder if she's single . . .*

Okay. It was never quite *that* bad.

But I definitely felt like things were tending in the wrong direction, and I was going to be happy to close this particular chapter in my gastronomic life—at least the part related to the creamy, pungent cheese.

Meg? Meg I wasn't at all sure about. After my surreal conversation with Henri in the public house, I vacillated between feelings of confusion, umbrage, and sheer disbelief. Whatever I thought I'd been thinking, I had to be wrong. *Right?* There was no way the woman was some kind of mysterious, ageless specter, floating around out there on a damn island.

Besides—nowhere in ghost lore did legions of the undead have a passion for goat cheese . . .

I know because I checked.

I also dug deeper into the personal history of Marguerite Steele. And surprise, surprise: her online biographies were woefully bereft of details. No date of birth. No information about family or other close connections. No records of any kind. It was like the woman didn't exist—except for her lengthy list of publications. And those all seemed to begin in earnest in 1982, when she collaborated with Laurent Bouchard on her first cookbook. I was no math whiz, but even I could do that calculus. If Meg had been writing and publishing books and articles since the decade I was born, that had to make her at least . . . sixty something.

Impossible.

I'd spent enough time with her in close proximity to know she couldn't be a day over . . . well . . . far less than that. Her presentation made her look much more mature than she probably was. She barely looked thirty, much less sixty-something.

It was some kind of damn paradox, to be sure. One I'd never be able to figure out while standing in the dark hanging film.

Once I had all nine of the rolls of film I'd shot so far processed and dried, I packed up my gear and made the short trip back north to the Champlain Islands. I'd brought a decent negative printer with me so I could generate test strips from each of our sessions. Those would be good enough quality for us to review the images and identify the shots she liked the best. I could do the final adjustments later, once I got back to Philadelphia. I just prayed there'd be images meeting her approval from each shoot, so I wouldn't have to recreate any of those damn dishes again.

It was while I was reviewing the contact prints I'd made that I noticed something odd. At the end of each cooking session, I took care to shoot several test images, just to be sure lighting and framing were optimal. Invariably, Meg would be moving in and out of each scene, fussing over some detail or correcting my placement of something like a damn sprig of chervil. It drove me nuts at first, and we had several lively arguments about my need for her to stand the fuck back and let me work. She largely ignored my protests—as usual—and I finally just gave up on entreating her to stay out of the damn shots. But looking at them now, I was stunned to discover that Meg didn't show up in any of the photos—not even the ones I remembered having our most energetic disagreements about.

She just wasn't there. Not in the background. Not anywhere.

What the serious fuck?

Making myself crazy trying to find an explanation was getting me no place. I resolved to do the unthinkable: ask her about it. After all, what was the worst that could happen? She could order me off her damn island? Tell me I'm *une idiote* . . . again? Pummel me with a log of goat cheese?

I had to stop and think about that last possibility a bit. It almost sounded . . . appealing.

Yeah. I needed to get off this damn aquatic merry-go-round . . .

> "If time, so fleeting, must like humans die,
> let it be filled with good food and good
> talk, and then embalmed in the perfumes of
> conviviality."
>
> –M.F.K. Fisher

Laurent was my salvation during those first years after Camille's death.

Wracked with grief and despair, I had retreated to my home on the island and refused to see anyone—including family members. They all protested mightily and for great duration, but I remained unmoved. The only exception I made to my determined isolation occurred after my parents were tragically killed in an automobile accident. They'd been visiting relatives in Montreal over Christmas, and were driving back to their hotel in a snowstorm when my father hit an icy patch of road on Boulevard Saint-Charles, about three blocks from their hotel. He skidded into the path of an oncoming city bus. They were killed instantly.

Laurent was the unhappy bearer of this news—and he alone accompanied me to New York City for their final arrangements and funeral mass at Church of the Ascension on the Upper West Side. I knew as I gazed at the grand east window with its bold depiction of the ascension of Christ that I would never again leave my island sanctuary. That day I took final leave of my parents—and of all surviving members of Camille's family.

Only Laurent refused to bend to my will. Throughout life, his was the only vein of stubbornness that came close to running as deep as my own. He delighted in showing up at my door, always without notice, and usually without agenda. And he would stay with me for days on end—often not speaking at all if that was my wish. But always tending to me in his characteristically fussy way.

It was during one such visit that Laurent telegraphed that he'd endured quite enough of my moribund behavior.

"*Assez!* It's time to end this protracted season of mourning, Meg."

I looked at him impassively.

"How long, in your view, should such a season last?"

"*Ne m'ennuies pas avec ça.*"

"I am not trying to *annoy* you, Laurent. I have not consulted any guidelines for the appropriate duration of grief."

"I understand that, *chère amie*. But it has been years. You cannot continue in this way."

I did not tell him that I'd begun debating a version of that same thought myself. He was right: I could no longer continue as I was. And I was inching closer to my own idea about what form an acceptable resolution might take.

But I was not ready to share it with him—or with anyone.

Laurent had been sitting at my kitchen table, drinking strong coffee and leafing through one of my many folders of recipes. He held up a sheet of paper.

"Where did you find this one?" he asked.

"What is it?"

He scanned the page. "A cassoulet made with white beans, chicken, pancetta, and rosemary."

I brushed it off. "It's just something I came up with—a summer alternative to the heavier dish, using lighter meats and seasonal herbs."

"You created this?"

"Oui."

He lifted the folder. "And the rest of these, too?"

"Oui. Why does this surprise you?"

He shook his head. "It does not *surprise* me. It stuns me."

I found his reaction curious.

"Pourquoi?"

"Because you express interest in next to nothing. You wander around this island like you're in some kind of daze. You barely string more than three words together—when you deign to speak at all. And yet, you've created all of these recipes? And done what with them? Filed them into folders that, presumably, no one will ever see, much less try? It makes no sense, Meg."

"Perhaps not to you. I do not create them for dissemination. I make them for . . ." I did not finish my thought.

"For Camille?" Laurent knew me better than I knew myself.

I dropped my eyes. *"Oui.* For her."

"She cannot taste them."

It took an effort to blunt the flash of anger I felt at his retort.

"Are you angry with me?" he asked.

"Oui."

"Good. Laurent closed the folder. "Anger is at least a sign that you are still alive—as are these incredible creations. They are brimming with life. And with a fire and zest for living that still burn within you, Meg. *Listen to them.* Heed them. Lay your obsession with Camille's death to rest, once and for all."

I was ready to end his determined cross-examination. I knew the quickest way to do so was to feign agreement.

"*D'accord*. I will think about it."

That seemed to satisfy him.

He stayed on with me several more days, and talked endlessly about his evolving ideas for how we might cobble the recipes together and submit them for publication. He was persuaded they would find a ready audience, and the exercise would serve as a springboard to facilitate my reentry to engagement with the outside world.

I listened to his unceasing bouts of ardent brainstorming politely, but with perfect indifference.

The truth was, I had already plunged deep into my own plans for how the next and final chapter of my life should unfold.

> ". . . we felt as if we had seen the far shores of another world. We were drunk with the land breeze that blew from it, and the sure knowledge that it lay waiting for us."
>
> –M.F.K. Fisher

I wish I could say that all the hours Meg and I had spent together in virtual isolation on her unearthly damn island led her to relax her reserve a bit. Lighten up. Become less persnickety and fractious. Be more open and self-revealing. More authentic and less controlled.

Not a chance.

If anything, Meg appeared to stiffen her mostly inhospitable demeanor—along with her backbone. Our verbal exchanges devolved into arguments about . . . well . . . just about everything. My flame was too high. My *brunoise* was woefully uneven. My alcohol was not sufficiently burned off. My pasta water wasn't salted "like the ocean." The rib bones of my rack of lamb were not cleanly Frenched. You name it. If there were any entry-level mistakes a fledgling chef could make, I was sure to make them.

Thrice.

I knew no way to account for her increasing irascibility. In my experience, the familiarity with one another we'd been achieving should've led her to become at least quasi-cordial. But instead, she retreated further behind her wall of reserve and indifference—except when it came to pointing out my cascading culinary deficiencies. The only area where I managed to meet or possibly exceed her expectations was apparent from her review of my written summaries of our goat cheese-infused cooking excursions. Those she tacitly approved—generally without comment, but always with a nearly imperceptible cluck of her tongue.

I decided to take her to task for it. The truth was, I was becoming addicted to her scowls. It was a lot like acting out in grade school to gain attention from the hot-looking teacher who ignored you otherwise.

"Go ahead and admit it, Meg."

"Admit?" She was perplexed by my request. "Admit what?"

I grinned at her. "Admit that as much as you hate my cooking, you think my writing is sublime."

"Sublime?"

"*Oui*. Su-bleem." I quoted her.

She glared at me.

"So? Come on, Meg. Admit it. It won't kill you."

I thought I saw something flicker across her face—some unreadable reaction to my entreaty.

"I do not hate your cooking," she said, with exaggerated coolness.

"All evidence to the contrary."

"Why are you being so . . . irascible?"

"Moi?" I pointed at myself with a dramatic flourish. "Don't you have that backwards?"

"Non. And I am *not* irascible. Nor do I hate your cooking. That is a ridiculous and inaccurate assessment."

The intensity of her denial was punctuated by an ominous

rumble of thunder. We had finished our quota of recipes for the day, and the detritus of my efforts was still strewn about her normally pristine kitchen. Because we had planned to prepare five dishes that day, instead of our customary four, I'd arranged for Henri to fetch me at 6 p.m. instead of our customary time, two hours earlier. I had already determined that once we'd finished our work for the day, I was going to make an opportunity to ask her about some of the mysteries I'd uncovered about her . . . well . . . about *her.* I figured asking her to review the contact prints with me would be a good segue into querying her about why she never showed up in any of the images—and how it was possible that she'd published her first cookbook in 1982. If it pissed her off? Well? I had little to lose. And it wouldn't be the first time my impertinence would cause her to bristle with impatience.

It was barely five o'clock, but the sky had steadily been growing darker. Neither of us had paid much attention to it until it was time to photograph the completed dishes and I realized that I needed to add more background light. It was when we heard the first rumble of thunder, followed in quick succession by a bright flash and another rolling boom, that we looked at each other with concern.

"That doesn't sound too good," I offered.

"Non," she agreed. She looked out the window at the lake. It was roiling and lashing the shore with angry waves. *"Ce n'est pas bon signe."*

I didn't need for her to translate her comment. It was pretty clear what she meant.

"Yeah. It looks like you might be stuck with me for a while."

"Coincée? I wouldn't say I'm stuck with you."

"You wouldn't?"

"Non." She actually smiled. "You still need to clean up this mess."

One step forward. Two steps back. That's how things went with our twisted *pas de deux.*

But I had to admit . . . she looked pretty damn good when she smiled.

We fell into our normal routine, clearing and stacking bowls, utensils, and baking sheets. All the while, the storm outside gained steam. Rain was beating against the windows of the kitchen with an intensity I had not witnessed before—and the onset of these sudden storms had not been uncommon during my stay in the islands.

After a particularly loud crash of thunder, I shot Meg a worried look.

"I'm not feeling super confident about this."

"About what?"

"This storm. It seems more violent than usual."

"Summer storms are often this way." She folded her dishtowel and placed it on the countertop. "They pop up suddenly and dissipate just as quickly. It will blow over soon. Would you like to sit on the porch and watch it move through the islands?"

Her offer surprised me. Meg had never invited me into another area of her home. It felt—personal. Like I'd passed some kind of test and was finally being permitted a glimpse behind the impenetrable curtain she wore like a second skin.

"Sure. I mean . . . is it safe?"

"To watch the storm?" she asked.

"No. To be outside?"

"Oui. It's miles away from here. There is no danger."

"How can you be sure?"

"Because I've been here on this island for . . ." she hesitated. "A *long* time. I can tell when the storms are a threat and when they are just *une tracasserie."*

I was intrigued by her explanation.

A flash of lightning so white it illuminated the room was followed in short order by a rumble of thunder that shook the stemware on a nearby shelf.

"And this one is just . . . what did you call it?"

"*Une petite tracasserie.* An annoyance." She smiled. *"Oui."*

I was pretty sure Meg was being too blasé about the intensity of the storm, but I decided not to argue with her. After all . . . she'd lived there "a long time."

"Okay, then. Lead on."

I collected the envelope containing the contact prints from my backpack before following her along a short hallway that led to a broad, enclosed porch that ran the width of the entire north side of the house. It had an expansive view of the lake, all the small islands to the north, and a clear line of sight to the Canadian border. And it gave us a ringside view of the storm, making its slow and protracted way across the lake. As Meg had predicted, it was easily ten miles or so north of us and moving due east.

Meg sat down on a settee and waved me toward a large wicker chair facing the view.

"Would you like something to drink?"

Her offer surprised me. It wasn't like Meg to be so attentive to courtesies.

"Sure." I was tempted to ask, *Whattaya got?* But thought better of it.

She got up from her seat and walked to a small cabinet that sat snugly against the back wall of the porch. I heard her preparing something, but I had no idea what it was. I was surprised when she came back carrying a small tumbler of some amber-colored liquid. She held it out to me.

"I hope you like cognac?"

As it happened, I did. Quite a lot. But I noticed that she held only one glass.

"Thank you. This looks perfect. Aren't you joining me?"

"No. I . . . don't usually partake."

I took a small sip. It was delightful. Fruity and slightly smoky. It tasted expensive, which was hardly surprising.

"This is phenomenal. What is it?"

"It's . . ." She stopped herself. "It's old. It belonged to my parents, so it's been here a while."

"Really?" I held the glass up toward the windows to give the liquid a closer examination just as a flash of lightning lit up the entire porch. The liquid was a sensuous dark caramel color—practically shimmering inside the crystal tumbler. "How old? It tastes pretty extraordinary."

"It's Rémy Martin Louis XIII. A very good one, I believe."

Good? Hell. The stuff was like liquid fucking gold. It had to be at least fifty years old. I was impressed.

"Your parents had a taste for expensive hooch."

She actually smiled. "My father did. He was rather a snob about it, too."

I nearly quipped that it must've been a family characteristic, but managed to stop myself.

Marguerite noticed.

"Was there something you wanted to say?" Her eyes looked amused.

"I think you probably can intuit it just fine without assistance from me."

"I fear you are correct."

"That your father wasn't the only snob in the family?"

"Oui."

I narrowed my eyes as I considered her smug expression. *What was happening here?*

"Are we having some kind of breakthrough?" I asked her. "Or am I already hazy from a single sip of this vintage elixir?"

"Only you can be the judge of that."

Okay . . . was she actually flirting with me?

Impossible.

I had to be misreading her tone.

More thunder rolled in the distance. Rain was still lashing the house, but it wasn't as violent as it had been earlier. I took another cautious sip of the fabled cognac.

In for a penny, in for a pound. I picked up the folder of contact prints and passed it to her.

"I thought we might review these images from our first two weeks. I finally got a chance to process the film on Saturday."

Meg took the folder from me and withdrew the stack of photos. She took her time flipping through them.

"These are very good, Kip. You did a commendable job."

"You sound surprised."

She looked up at me. “Do I? I don’t mean to. I expected them to be perfect.”

Perfect? Had she actually uttered the word “perfect” in context with something I did? This unlikely event and the epic storm had to be evidence that hell was, in fact, freezing over.

Or maybe, conversely, it was beginning to thaw . . .

I finished my drink and extended the glass toward her.

“Would it be terribly unseemly to ask for a refill?”

“Unseemly?” She stood up to take the glass from me. “Probably. But I won’t hold it against you.”

“No? I’m tempted to ask what’s on the list of things you would hold against me.”

“Oh, that. It’s fairly short and is mostly limited to your sustained and loquacious lack of respect for my featured ingredient.”

Fucking goat cheese. Of course.

“Oh, come on,” I argued. “I haven’t complained about it that much, have I?”

“Shall I count the ways?”

“Can you?”

She handed me my refill and reclaimed her seat on the settee.

“Let’s see.” She crossed her legs. I had to fight not to stare at them. “Sour logs of crumbly white clay. As stale smelling as a drunk’s balls—that one was my personal favorite, by the way. Perfect for grouting tile. Tastes like something raked up in a barnyard. A noxious byproduct my body can’t process. Uncommonly *b-a-a-a-d.*” She smiled brightly at me. “How am I doing?”

Her smile was disarming. It took years off her countenance.

Now I really wondered what the fuck was going on with her.

“Pretty good,” I said grudgingly. “I guess I have been kind of an ass.”

“Oh, I wouldn’t say *kind of.*”

“Touché. But I’ve had reason to reconsider my earlier opinions. It’s become an acquired taste.”

"That *can* happen," Meg agreed.

"Can it?"

Her eyes met mine, but she didn't reply. After a moment, she dropped her gaze and resumed looking at the photos.

I felt off balance. And confused as hell. My mind was racing, and the rest of me was following right along in its wake.

What the fuck is happening here? I know I'm not imagining this.

Had I awakened in some alternate reality where this indifferent ice queen was suddenly playing hopscotch with me as if I'd just hit on her in a bar?

I needed answers—before I did something profoundly stupid and got my ass tossed outside to have to wait in the rain for Henri to show up.

"May I ask you something, Meg?"

"*Oui.*" She didn't look up.

"Henri told me that he'd been ferrying supplies out here to you for more than thirty years. Is that true?"

Meg's expression changed. It took her a while to reply.

"Why do you need to know this?"

I noted that she didn't say, *Of course not.*

"Because I see no way that can be possible. Yet he was very clear about it. He also said that, before his death, he'd brought your previous collaborator, Laurent Bouchard, out here for at least as many years. You published your first cookbook with Laurent in 1982—forty-one years ago. Before I was born. Are these things also true?"

Meg's expression was changing faster than the shapes of the storm clouds rolling across the sky outside the windows.

"You've been busy." Her tone was unreadable. "Any other questions?"

"Just two. I've never seen you eat anything—and I see no evidence here that you ever do."

She waited for me to continue, and when I didn't, she gave me the same measured look.

"You said two more questions."

"Okay. Those photos?" I gestured toward the folder she held.

"You don't appear in *any* of them—not in any of the setup shots I took where you were constantly underfoot, reaching into the frame to fuss with details of the compositions. So tell me, Meg," I leaned toward her. "What the serious fuck is going on with you?"

I didn't know what to expect from her by way of a response. Was she going to tell me I was delusional? That I had a suspicious mind and overactive imagination? That I was being rude and impertinent? That digging into her personal life was base and prurient? That I was fired and needed to get the hell out of her house?

I expected any of those responses from her. What I didn't expect is what she actually did say.

"So. It appears you've found me out."

"I'm not sure I know what that means."

She got up and walked back to the liquor cabinet. When she returned, she set the bottle of Rémy Martin Louis XIII on top of a small table beside my chair.

I looked at her with surprise. "What's this for?"

"Short answer? The truth."

"You think I'll need this?"

"I think you'll need at *least* this, Kip."

"Okay . . ."

She took a long slow breath. "With apologies to *David Copperfield*, I will begin my life at the beginning of my life. Which is to say that I was born to Patrick and Isabelle Overleaux Steele in Montreal . . ." she paused, "on August 1, 1925."

"Nineteen . . ." I couldn't make sense of her words.

"You heard me correctly. Ninety-eight years ago."

"But that's . . ."

"*Impossible?* Yes. It should be. But it isn't, I assure you."

"I don't understand." I felt like I'd gotten stuck on one of those horrible carnival rides—the ones that swing you around in wild arcs until you lose your sense of what's up and what's down.

"Neither did I at first. I thought it was some kind of cruel joke—another one, carried out because fate had not yet done enough to destroy what remained of my life."

"So you're telling me that you're . . ."

"Dead?" she offered.

"Well . . . yeah. I mean . . . are you telling me you're some kind of ghost?"

"I'm *not* dead, Kip. I assure you. I'm just not really *alive.* Not in the sense that you are—or Henri is. Or any of the other people in this don't-ask-don't-tell island community are."

"I think I'm losing my mind here."

"That's all right," she said softly. "I nearly lost mine for the first few decades. Then I learned to live with it. I had to because I knew I could never die with it."

She reached across the space that separated us and touched the back of my hand. Even in my dazed state, I noticed that her hand felt awfully supple and warm for one belonging to some kind of ghoul.

I turned my hand over beneath hers and squeezed her fingers. To my amazement, she didn't pull her hand away. She let me sit there and hold onto it, like a drowning man grasping a lifeline.

"What are you telling me?" I tried not to sound as desperate as I felt. "*Why are you telling me?*"

"Maybe I'm tired of hiding the truth. Or maybe I just wanted you to know. You, specifically."

"Me?" In the midst of so many unbelievable things, I found that statement to be the least credible of them all. "Why would you care what I think?"

She lifted her chin. "Why do you think I might care?"

I looked at her. Her face held an expression I'd only seen a few, fleeing times—quick glances she'd shot me when she thought I wasn't looking—and always after we'd exchanged some exaggerated repartee related to some colossal mistake I'd made and we'd had to waste time troubleshooting a resolution.

For the first time I realized that I hadn't been alone in thinking there'd been some kind of primal spark igniting between us.

Just my luck, my tortured mind chimed in. *You finally meet the right woman and she's . . . what the hell was she? Undead? Some otherworldly apparition that still managed to be tactile in all the right ways—not to mention, completely hot as fuck?*

Yeah. Just my luck.

"Bummer." I kept hold of her hand. "So, does this mean you can walk through walls and things?"

Meg actually smiled. "Alas, no. I still have to use doors."

"What *happened* to you?"

She gave a bitter-sounding laugh and gestured at the bottle of her father's cognac.

"Drink up, Kip. This might take a while."

> "Children and old people and the parents in between should be able to live together, in order to learn how to die with grace, together."
>
> –M.F.K. Fisher

I don't even remember how I got back to my hotel that night. I fell into bed in a near stupor and fought my way through a restless night full of twisted and surreal dreams. Or were they mad delusions brought into frighteningly bold relief by the mind-blowing contours of Marguerite's tale of love and loss—and her ill-fated attempts to end her decades of suffering by taking her own life?

Meg explained how both she and Camille had been stricken by polio during the 1952 epidemic that swept the country. She said I probably had noticed her limp, but noted that the real damage she carried with her was buried deep inside.

She described how she woke up wet, disoriented and disheveled on the rocks along the south end of her island, after swimming far out into the lake and letting the waves take her.

"I was finished with a life of sadness and loss. I could no longer function. There was nothing left for me. I had lost Camille, and I knew that life held nothing for me but more of the same. So after a decade of misery, I resolved to end it."

But drowning didn't end her life—or at least, not completely.

"What does that mean?" I asked her.

"I didn't know myself at first. It took me a while to understand what had changed—that I wasn't really alive. I didn't sleep. I didn't need to eat. And I couldn't kill myself, no matter how many ways I tried." She looked at me sadly. "And believe me, Kip—I tried. This nightmare was compounded when I discovered that I couldn't leave my island prison, either." She gave me a bitter smile. "Laurent thought I'd lost my mind when I tried to explain it to him. The only way I was finally able to convince him was to take a boning knife from the block and plunge it into my abdomen."

"Dear God . . ."

"Poor Laurent nearly fainted until he realized that I was unhurt, and there wasn't even any blood. Although, in retrospect, he could've been more shocked that I returned the knife to the block without washing it . . ."

I wasn't used to this side of Meg—the droll, self-deprecating woman who seemed to have no difficulty poking fun at her predicament. But I guessed she'd had a lot of time to cultivate her particular brand of dark humor.

We ended up sitting together on the settee, holding hands, while she told me her sad story of unrequited love and loss. She took her time with the telling, too—allowing me the space I needed to try to process all she was revealing. Although I was sure that feat was going to take far longer than the hours we'd spent together talking about it all.

"I can imagine that losing Laurent last year was a great blow to you."

"It was," she agreed. "I was devastated. He was my oldest and dearest friend. When he was gone, I was truly alone in a way I had never been before."

"So, no one else knows about your . . ." I wasn't sure what to call it. "Predicament?"

"C'est une bonne description." She laughed and gave my fingers a squeeze. "I've never thought about calling it a 'predicament.' I like it. It sounds . . . lighter. More casual. Like something I should overcome with more time and effort."

"I'm sorry, Meg. I don't mean to make light of this . . . situation."

"Don't apologize. I'm relieved you didn't flee and order up a butterfly net."

"I wouldn't do that." I bumped her shoulder. "Even though you'd probably look great wearing that, too."

She looked amused. "You think so?"

I nodded. "Not even a question."

"I have no defense for you." She shook her head. "But it's hopeless, Kip. *I* am hopeless. There is no future here. Not for either of us. There is only more of this—everything creeping toward the same unhappy outcome."

"Why does it have to be unhappy?" I hadn't known until I was on the verge of losing her how desperately I wanted to stay with her.

"I lost Camille, *ma chère*. I lost Laurent. I don't want to lose you, too."

"You won't."

"But I will. Don't you see? There is no other outcome for me. For us."

I had no counterargument. No ready way to try to change her mind. I knew better than anyone what a will of steel she had.

I laughed at my own, bitter joke. *Meg had been well named indeed.*

"My agent," she said.

I was confused by her statement.

"You asked me if anyone besides Laurent knew about me."

"Your *agent* knows?"

"Oui."

"Doesn't she think that's . . . *crazy?*"

"My agent?" Meg laughed. "I could be out here feasting on the blood of virgins for all she knows. She doesn't care about anything as long as I keep publishing and she gets her fifteen percent."

I had to agree with her on that one. Agents were a peculiar breed.

"What are we going to do?" I knew I probably sounded as desperate as I was beginning to feel.

"There is nothing for us to do, Kip. You will leave and go back to your life, and I will stay here. That's all there is."

"That can't be all there is. I refuse to accept it."

She stroked my face. "You have no choice but to accept it. None of this can be changed."

"But I can touch you. I can feel you. You are real—not imagined. Not spectral. You are flesh and blood. Just like me."

"Not like you, *mon amour.* I can never belong to you because I am a hostage to fate. To time. And will be so for eternity."

"We don't know that."

"We don't ever know what we don't know. We only know what is. And this is what is."

She leaned her head against my shoulder, and I wrapped my arms around her.

"I won't give up on us. I can't."

"You must. We have right now. Let it be enough."

"A lifetime wouldn't be enough." I kissed her. It was gentle at first—a sweet, shared exploration. But it escalated rapidly into something more intense and passionate. I didn't want it to end. I thought if it didn't, if we stayed exactly like we were, I could keep her with me. In the same way we could take other mixtures of unlikely elements and create things that were harmonious. Magical. Things that would endure.

Just like all those infernal goat cheese recipes of hers.

But it wasn't to be. Meg stopped us.

"We can't."

Her sad expression told me this was an argument I'd never win.

"You want me to leave you?"

"Yes. Because I can never leave you. *Please*. Please don't make me suffer that fate, too."

So I left her.

She walked outside with me and stood at the top of the walkway. She stayed there while Henri pushed the boat away from her dock and began the slow journey back to the mainland. I stood in the stern, riding the swells and watching her figure grow smaller, until she was enveloped by the swirling mist and declining light.

Nothing had changed, and everything had changed.

Amid so many things I still could not comprehend, only one thing was clear: we each had been cursed by the same fate.

> "In general, I think, human beings are happiest at table when they are very young, very much in love, or very alone."
>
> –M.F.K. Fisher

I stood and watched until Henri's boat disappeared from view. Once the realization sunk in that Kip was truly gone, I was at a loss about what to do with myself. I wandered the island aimlessly, staring with blank eyes at its familiar prospects—each site that once had held such resonance and meaning for me. Cliffs and coves that once formed the boundaries of my small world now surrounded me like prison walls.

Now I looked at them with despair.

What had happened to me? I was behaving like someone I didn't recognize. I had never once thought twice about anyone besides Camille—not while she was alive, and not since I'd been . . . consigned to this unhappy fate—locked inside some incomprehensible state of not quite being alive, but not quite dead, either. For the first time, it seemed intolerable to me. *I was angry about it.* I didn't choose to end up this way: a hostage to unrequited passion.

Did I?

Or was I, in fact, a willing hostage to the fate I'd carved out for myself? A prisoner of my own misguided and failed aspirations? Had I actively chosen to wither and dry on a twisted vine of self-flagellation?

I began to think I was nearing the truth. And the truth was more spine-chilling than I could have imagined. "Waste and horror," F. Scott Fitzgerald had written about his own failed life, "what I might have been and done that is lost, spent, gone, dissipated, unrecapturable."

Waste and horror summarized my predicament exactly.

Never before, during my decades of isolation, had I felt so alone. Never before had I wanted so desperately to find release from the captivity I'd passively accepted as my fate—not even in my grief after Laurent had left me for good. I had been a good student of my mentor, M.F. K. Fisher. "I think we grieve forever," she'd written. "But that goes for love too, fortunately for us all."

And never before had I allowed myself to consider that I might one day feel pangs of—attraction . . . *of passion* . . . for another person. For another woman. For Kip. It stunned me at first. I resisted it because it felt impossible—not to mention, disloyal to the memory of Camille. But as the weeks had gone by and our interactions had become more relaxed—and flirtatious—the realization of my increasing attachment to her grew impossible to deny. And admitting the truth of my own feelings for Kip was compounded by the realization that she was entertaining the same ideas about me.

There was no way I could allow the situation to devolve any further. There was no possibility of a happy outcome for either of us. And it made no sense to me to prolong the agony of a vexatious conclusion. Our work was nearly completed, and there seemed little reason to put off the inevitable.

I was dejected and miserable. Finally giving up on finding any answers outside, I retreated to the sanctuary of my kitchen—the only place I'd ever found solace from my pain and grief. I sat down at the table and pulled over the folder of manuscript notes Kip had compiled on all the recipes we'd worked on together during her weeks with me. Reading her notes and clever asides containing tips and techniques for the average cooks who one day would be attempting to cook these dishes at home was a delight for me. She was a good writer with a lively and conversational voice. It was easy to understand why she came so highly recommended. I soon became lost in reading through the pages and pages of recipe notes.

It was while turning a page that I cut my finger. It was a fairly deep cut, too, and was bleeding.

"Merde!"

It hurt like the dickens and I continued to curse in a most unladylike fashion.

As I dabbed at the blood from the tip of my index finger, I noticed the random sheet of thicker paper that had been inserted into the stack. It had been this one that had caused my injury. I picked it up and examined it.

Whipped Dill Goat Cheese Breakfast Buns with Eggs Over Easy.

Breakfast Buns? *What on earth?* This certainly wasn't one of *my* recipes. And it sounded . . . ridiculous and overwrought with its fried, spiralized potato nests and sliced cucumbers. How had this ungodly creation ended up in the manuscript of my cookbook?

Kip.

Obviously she had stuck this into the book to annoy me . . . It was exactly the kind of thing she did, virtually nonstop.

It was while I was running warm water over my fingertip and ransacking the unused medicine cabinet for a plaster that I realized with a shock that I was bleeding. *Bleeding.* I was hurt. I had sustained an injury that required attention. And it hurt. It hurt like nothing I had felt in decades. That revelation was quickly supplanted by another one of even greater magnitude.

My stomach growled.

I was . . . hungry.

What on earth had happened to me?

I had an inkling that something had changed. Something monumental. I gave up on finding a bandage and walked to the refrigerator to seek out something to test my hypothesis. All that confronted me was goat cheese. *A lot of it.* I pulled out a hunk of it and pinched off a small bite. I could taste it. I could eat it. And it was . . . well . . . *goaty.* I smiled as I chewed.

Maybe Kip was right about this entire project?

There was one more test. *The lake.* Could I now leave my island prison and wade into the water? Had I, indeed, been freed from my curse?

I left the house and headed for the path that led to the water.

Depending upon the outcome of that last experiment, I might need to make other plans for tomorrow. And for all the tomorrows after that.

"When shall we live if not now?"

–M.F.K. Fisher

I managed to finish packing my bags before dragging myself downstairs for a final breakfast in the hotel's small dining room. All the usual diners were there. I waved at the round couple from Quebec who always sat at a square table near the front window, babbling away in French throughout their entire meal. They'd been staying at the hotel longer than me, and had explained that they were in the islands visiting their daughter, who'd just had her first child, a girl named Sophie.

"Bonjour, Kip," Rene called out. His wife, Monique, beamed at me. *"Que fais-tu aujourd'hui?* More cooking?"

"Good morning, you two. Sadly, no. I am leaving today."

"Mais pourquoi? Is your work finished so soon?" They appeared genuinely sad at my news.

"No. Well. Yes. It is. Sort of." I waved my hand in frustration. "We finished sooner than expected."

"We will be very sorry to have you go." Monique looked like she meant it.

"I will miss seeing the two of you as well. I hope you enjoy the rest of your time with your granddaughter."

"Merci." Rene raised his teacup in a salute. "Have a safe journey home. Perhaps we will see you here again one day?" He sounded hopeful.

I didn't have the heart to tell him that was about as likely as the sun coming up in the west.

"Perhaps, my friends. Be well."

My server arrived to read me the morning special. I stopped her midstream and explained that I wasn't very hungry and would just have coffee and juice. She looked somewhat crestfallen, but accepted my request—grudgingly, I thought—and scurried off toward the kitchen.

The morning paper was neatly folded and sitting on the corner of my table. I picked it up and scanned its headlines, more to distract myself from my misery than because I cared about the news. The Annual Duct Tape Regatta was set to take place on Saturday. The article featured photos of last year's winner, a cardboard and duct tape replica of something that vaguely resembled the PT 109, replete with torpedoes and American flags.

I supposed you had to be there . . .

The local rescue squad was hosting a barbecue dinner at Hackett's Orchard. There would be maple creemees and pony rides for the kids. Musical entertainment would be provided by Reefer & Skeeter, a Jamaican steel band from Winooski.

Winooski?

I set the newspaper aside. None of this was helping my headache—or my heartache.

The server arrived with the coffee—and a breakfast tray containing several plates of steaming . . . something.

"What is all this?" I asked with surprise.

"It's on the house. Our guest chef made it special this morning."

She began unloading plates. To be fair, it looked pretty upscale for such a humble establishment. There was some kind of spiralized potato nest that had been fried to a crispy golden brown. It was served with sides of sliced cucumbers, a perfectly fried egg, and a small bowl of some kind of whipped cheese spread topped with fresh dill.

Wait a minute . . .

I took a cautious bite of the cheese spread.

Son of a bitch. It was fucking goat cheese. *Whipped goat cheese.* With dill.

This wasn't some random breakfast special. This was the same goddamn bogus recipe I'd stuck into Meg's manuscript a week ago. *What the hell?* Who was this mysterious guest chef?

I looked frantically around the restaurant—and that's when I saw her, casually leaning against the doorframe that led to the kitchen, with her arms crossed, watching me. She was wearing chef togs, and she looked . . . smug. *And happy.*

I started to get up, but she gestured for me to stay seated while she walked across the small dining room to join me. She pulled out a chair and sat down across from me.

"*You* are the guest chef?" I asked, stupidly.

"Oui." She said it so matter-of-factly, it was almost comical.

"But how did you . . ."

"Leave the island? Easy. I called Henri to come and pick me up."

"Meg."

"Oui?"

"How can you be here? What the hell changed?"

She reached across the table and began assembling my breakfast bun creation with its whipped goat cheese and dill.

"I was so bereft and distracted when you left, I didn't know what to do with myself. So I sat down at the table and began reading through all the manuscript notes you'd made on the dishes. That's when I managed to cut my finger on a thicker sheet of paper. I was irate. It stung like the dickens and bled all over one of the recipes. That was when I stopped and realized what had happened." She met my eyes. "I was *bleeding,* Kip. Do you understand?"

I stared at her open-mouthed, unable to comprehend what she was telling me.

"My finger was *bleeding.*" She held it up so I could see the finger cot covering it. "And the paper that cut me? It was this infernal recipe—the one you must've added to the manuscript."

"I thought you might find it long after we'd finished the project. I wanted to make you laugh."

"It did more than make me laugh. It somehow set me free." She held my gaze. "*You* set me free."

"I did?" I was still too stunned to string more than a few words together. All the colors of my world were changing right before my eyes.

Meg picked up a fork and cut into the dish she'd prepared for me.

"Other discoveries followed in quick succession."

"Like what?"

Well," she lifted a bite of the savory potato, cheese and egg mixture to her mouth. "I realized I was ravenous."

"Oh, my God, Meg. Does this mean you're . . ."

"Alive? I don't know." She put the forkful of food into her mouth and ate it. "You tell me."

I had a hard time not leaping across the table to grab her and howl out my surge of joy.

She smiled at me.

"You know what?" she asked in a sultry voice.

"What?" I croaked.

"This tastes pretty damn good. I think you might have a future in this business."

I laughed. "If only I knew someone who could help me get established."

"I know people. Let me see what I can do."

Right then, I had a few thoughts about some things she

could do. Things both of us could do. I leaned across the table toward her. She met me hallway, and we shared a kiss that was alive with a perfect blend of joy, longing, and a lingering tinge of goat cheese.

And Meg was right. It did taste pretty damn good.

ABOUT THE AUTHORS

ANNA BURKE is an award-winning author who holds an MFA from and teaches Creative Writing at Emerson College. She is a graduate of the Golden Crown Literary Society's Writing Academy, for which she was the inaugural recipient of the Sandra Moran Scholarship. Her writing interests include feminist retellings and queer fiction—and she takes joy in emotionally torturing her characters. She and her wife live with their spoiled pets in Massachusetts.

Novels by Anna Burke include *Compass Rose, Sea Wolf, Thorn, Nottingham, Spindrift, Night Tide,* and *In the Roses of Pieria* (The Blood Files, Book No. 1).

Twitter | @annaburkeauthor
Instagram | @annaburkeauthor
Facebook | facebook.com/annaburkeauthor/
Patreon | patreon.com/annaburkeauthor
Website | http://annahburke.com/

JENN ALEXANDER holds an MS in Counseling from the University of North Texas. She is a graduate of the Golden Crown Literary Society's Writing Academy, for which she was the recipient of the Sandra Moran Scholarship. A two-time winner of Golden Crown Literary Society Awards, she lives in Edmonton, Canada, with her two beautiful daughters and one sweet and amazing dog.

Novels by Jenn Alexander include *The Song of the Sea, Home,* and *Live it Out*. Her novel *Bloodline* will publish in April 2024.

Twitter | @jennalexwrites
Instagram | @jenn.alexander.writes
Facebook | facebook.com/jenn.alexander.313/
Website | http://jennalexander.ca/

JACOB BUDENZ is an accomplished queer writer, multi-disciplinary performer, educator, and witch with an MFA from the University of New Orleans and a BA from Johns Hopkins University whose work explores the intersections between otherness and the otherworldly. A 2020 winner of the Baker Innovative Projects Grant for *Simaetha: a Dreambaby Cabaret*, Jake has work in journals including *Slipstream, Taco Bell Quarterly, Baffling, Wussy Magazine*, and more, as well as in anthologies by Mason Jar Press and Lycan Valley publications.

Jake's short story collection *Tea Leaves* published in September 2023.

Twitter | @dreambabyjake
Instagram | @dreambabyjake
Website | http://jakebeearts.com/

VIRGINIA BLACK likes strong whiskey, loud music, and writing, though not necessarily in that order. When not penning dark speculative fiction, she is almost always reading. Born in California—where even the green is brown—Virginia escaped to the verdant grass and rain showers of the Pacific Northwest. She lives with her wife of more than twenty years and their savagely witty teenage daughter.

Virginia's debut novel, *Consecrated Ground*, is now available. Her novel *No Shelter but the Stars* will publish in January 2024.

Twitter | @virginiablk517
Instagram | @virginiablackwrites
Facebook | facebook.com/virginiablackwrites/
Website | http://virginiablackwrites.com/

CATHY PEGAU grew up in New York state reading horror, science fiction, and fantasy novels, and playing RPGs. Her science fiction romances have won RWA Fantasy, Futuristic, and

Paranormal (FF&P) Chapter Best Futuristic Romance and Best of the Best Prism Awards and a Golden Crown Literary Award for Science Fiction/Fantasy. She lives in Alaska with her spouse, two dogs, and numerous roaming moose.

Cathy's story, "In Speary Wood" is a prequel to *The Demon Equilibrium*, which was published by Bywater Books in 2021. Her novel *Blood Remains* will publish in May 2024.

Twitter | @cathy.pegau
Facebook | facebook.com/cathy.pegau/
Website | http://cathypegau.com/

ANN MCMAN is the author of twelve novels and two short story collections. She is a two-time Lambda Literary Award recipient, a six-time Independent Publisher (IPPY) medalist, a *Foreword Reviews* INDIES medalist, and a laureate of the Alice B. Foundation for her outstanding body of work. She is also the recipient of eleven Golden Crown Literary Society Goldie Awards for writing, book cover design, and volunteer service. She lives in Winston-Salem, North Carolina.

Novels and short story collections by Ann McMan include *Jericho, Aftermath, Goldenrod, Covenant, Dust, Galileo, Backcast, Hoosier Daddy, Festival Nurse, Beowulf for Cretins, The Big Tow, Dead Letters from Paradise, Three (plus one)*, and *Sidecar*. Her novel, *The Black Bird of Chernobyl* will publish in July 2024.

Twitter | @annmcman
Instagram | @mcmanann
Facebook | facebook.com/ann.mcman/
Website | http://annmcman.com/

A NOTE ON THE TYPE

The body of this book is set in Adobe Caslon Pro. William Caslon was an English gunsmith and designer of typefaces. In 1722 he created an extended set of serif typefaces that were based on seventeenth-century Dutch old style designs. Because of their remarkable practicality, Caslon's typefaces met with instant success. These, as well as all of their consecutive revivals, are referred to as Caslon. Among those revivals are two Adobe versions, called Adobe Caslon (1990) and Adobe Caslon Pro, which includes an extended character set.

Bywater Books believes that all people have the right to read or not read what they want—and that we are all entitled to make those choices ourselves. But to ensure these freedoms, books and information must remain accessible. Any effort to eliminate or restrict these rights stands in opposition to freedom of choice. Please join with us by opposing book bans and censorship of the LGBTQ+ community.

At Bywater Books, we are *all* stories.

We are committed to bringing the best of contemporary literature to an expanding community of readers. Our editorial team is dedicated to finding and developing outstanding writers who create books you won't want to put down.

For more information about Bywater Books, our authors, and our titles, please visit our website.

www.bywaterbooks.com

Printed in the USA
CPSIA information can be obtained
at www.ICGtesting.com
JSHW020746200923
48752JS00003B/4